THANK YOU F
THE ALGO

MW01201298

10p

STAFF
Editor-in-Chief: Alex Woodroe
Publisher: Matt Blairstone
Editor: Cameron Howard
Designer: Braulio Tellez

Associate editors: j ambrose, Sasha Brown, Emma Cole, Dany Melchor, Zachary Gillan, Bryce Meerhaeghe, Samir Sirk Morató, Jonathan Olfert, Kathleen Palm, Jessica Peter, Marissa van Uden, Kelsea Yu, Hazel Zorn

Cover art: Becca Snow
Inside art: Samir Sirk Morató

Content Warnings are available
at the end of this issue.
Please consult this list for any
particular subject matter you
may be sensitive to.

Visit our website at www.tenebrouspress.com.
First Printing, November 2023.
The characters and events portrayed in this work are fictitious.
Any similarity to real persons, living or dead, is coincidental
and not intended by the author.
Print ISBN: 978-1-959790-00-6
eBook ISBN: 978-1-959790-01-3

FICTION

POETRY & WEIRD FORMS

ART, COMICS & LOGIC PUZZLE

EDITORIAL

LETTER FROM THE EDITOR

||||||||||||||||||||||||||||||||||||||||||||||||||||||||||||||||||||||||||||||||||||||||||||||||||||||||||||||||||||||||||||||||||||||||||||||||||||||||||||||

W E'RE UNDER ATTACK. Artificial intelligence is threatening the livelihoods of writers, artists, and creative workers of all kinds. Generative AI programs such as ChatGPT and DALL-E are a pale imitation of the AI that classic Science Fiction stories warned us about, but their irresponsible development and exploitative use remain a cause for concern.

WE'RE FOCUSING ON THE REAL ISSUES. Fanciful comparisons to human learning and "clever" objections that yesterday's copyright laws don't explicitly restrict an emerging technology only serve to distract from the actual issues at the heart of the AI debate.

The most popular generative AI programs could not function the way they do if not for training on terabytes of data from the internet, much of it indiscriminately scraped from works owned by writers and artists without their consent. The development of these programs required art theft at an unprecedented scale; this is irrefutable.

Popular fiction magazines have been flooded with AI-generated submissions, low-quality content proliferated by tech blogs advertising it as an effortless get rich quick scheme. A deluge of AI-generated books have inundated online marketplaces, displacing legitimate self-publishing efforts from flesh-and-blood authors. And with AI-generated images available at the press of a button, it's never been harder for legitimate artists to secure fair compensation for their work. The material harm to creative workers is real.

WE'RE NOT ALONE. Creative workers are fighting back. Many genre magazines explicitly forbid AI-generated submissions. Independent publishers are taking firm stances, including anti-AI clauses in their contracts and committing to paying artists for cover art rather than using AI-generated images. Recognizing AI for the cross-discipline threat it is, the community is beginning to foster solidarity.

WE'RE PUTTING OUR MONEY WHERE OUR MOUTH IS. Every writer and artist featured in Thank You For Joining the Algorithm was paid for their work. Each signed a contract affirming that none of their work was AI-generated. The cover is a commissioned piece of original art, and the inside art was created through skillful manipulation of public domain and open source assets.

All proceeds from the sale of this publication—every cent remaining after printing, shipping, and taxes—will be donated to organizations that fight for the rights of human artists and pursue the regulation and limitation of generative AI in the arts.

The result is what you hold in your hands; a collective work of human creativity, unfiltered by AI interference. Your support helps keep art *human*. I can think of no greater cause than that.

||||||||||||||||||||||||||||||||||||||||||||||||||||||||||||||||||||||||||||||||||||||||||||||||||||||||||||||||||||||||||||||||||||||||||||||||||||||||||||||

Filtered

by Koji A. Dae

EVEN THOUGH I'M WAITING FOR THE CALL, I never expected my tablet to ring. I clear my throat, flip my hair to one side, and click ACCEPT.

The woman on my screen is gorgeous. Her red hair floats around her long face. Her lips are plump and smiling, and the smattering of freckles on her nose gives her the emotional affect of a lazy summer day.

Honestly, I'm thinking more about keywords to feed for some good porn later than the woman in front of me. Surely there are databases on the visual equivalent of sunshine sensations, but what about freckles? Spotted sex. Dappled, maybe?

"Lou?" the woman says. "It's nice to finally see you live."

"You too, Sybil."

She's not really seeing me. I've got the usual enhancements on. A curve to my tits, no mole on my chin, a flattening of my pores and a straightening of my lopsided smile. Her freckles probably aren't real, either. But it's a killer filter.

"Most people don't want to chat live these days," she says.

"Yeah." I agree because I don't know what to say and there's no time to think during synchronous calls.

We've been chatting for three weeks. After the first week, I got enough pings from my chat bot to start fielding her messages myself. She was funny from the get-go, full of sarcasm and memes. Not sure when she switched from bot to manual. Not sure I want to ask because I'll feel like an ass if I switched first. I'm pretty sure two weeks in, when she started suggesting a live call, it was really her. But it's possible her bot pings her on a yes and I was talking with AI for weeks. Either way, she was insistent. I put her off for a few days, but it was obvious I'd either have to vid or we'd go our separate ways.

Some people are weird about time and reality that way.

The problem is vid filters are always a few steps behind pics. In her pics, the space beneath her brows had been perfectly smooth, with just the smallest central protrusion of her nose. On vid, the illusion is ruined by the faint hint of two slits where her eyes must be.

Ugh. I shudder just thinking of the round wetness of eyes.

"I love your pic filters," she says, "Are you using Orion?"

I grin, hoping my lips stay in line with the filter. "It's a new one. Bathsheba. Heard of it?"

She hasn't, so I send her a link, even though the thought of being among the elite first users who find the next big hit is intoxicating.

She asks questions, telling me her opinions. She's better at it than I am. Probably has some service job that takes her away from her screen and keeps her practiced in this archaic art. Still, it's not unpleasant. Her voice has a rhythm and lilt to it, and the longer she talks, the more my mind releases, lubricated by her ease.

I check the clock when we hang up. Fifty-seven minutes. Longer than a flix. Seven more minutes than a work block. I turn off my screen. Sybil. She's like a filter that morphs time. The next big thing, at least for me.

◻

Most days I stay home, managing my team of six AI from my home computer, but at least once a week I have to go into the office for planning meetings. My work is just three subway stops away, but I put on lash magnets to close my eyes to narrow slits and cover my face with large sunglasses. I wrap a scarf around my too-flat hair, even in the heat of summer.

Most people give the same consideration, but as I walk down the street, trying to give them privacy by keeping my narrowed gaze on the sidewalk, I glimpse hints of their imperfections. They seem flat compared to the avatars I've grown used to. Their necks are too short and their shoulders have the wrong slope. Even when they wear gloves, their hands seem off. But the worst is their eyes.

One of my coworkers insists on going natural. I have to look into her round orbs as she gives presentations, and see the wetness of her nostrils when she raises her five-fingered hand to ask questions.

It's hell.

But I get to come home and get online with Sybil. She calls after I've made dinner, and we chat while eating together. Sometimes there's vid, and sometimes just audio. Honestly, I like the audio chats better. Whenever we vid, I get this lump in my throat that she'll move too fast and the filter will fall. I'll see a pimple or the roundness of her eyes, and the spell will be broken. Because she's too good to be true.

"Do you still use your prompter?" Sybil asks one night while I'm eating a reheated Mac and cheese.

I panic and look at the corner of my tablet for help.

Of course not. I love our authentic talks.

Yes, is that a problem?

Prompters help conversations flow more naturally. They should be used in every interaction.

None of the answers seem quite right. But with Sybil, "yeah" always seems to suffice.

"How much?"

"I dunno," I say. "Maybe half the time, maybe less."

"Ever voice bot me?"

My stomach drops. Not because I've done it, but because now I realize she might have.

"Not yet," I tease.

"Look, you want to drop the filters?"

I tap over to my profile. My chat bots have found three people they recommend I try manual chats with. But if I switch to one of them, how long will it be before they suggest dropping filters? Everyone except me seems to think going unfiltered builds intimacy. I consider adding another search to my chat-bot filters to get rid of the need to go bare. But for Sybil, it's too late.

"Yeah, sure."

◻

The good thing about flix and chill is the chill part. For all our advancements, I've yet to figure out an electronic equivalent to cuddling and kissing. The actual sex part is rarely better than masturbating, but everything leading up to it is worth a little reality.

We decide to meet at her place, half because I like my privacy and half because my apartment is a room with a shared kitchen and bathroom. She's got her own studio.

I shave and apply a layer of spray foundation. It smooths out the worst of my humanity but it's nothing compared to a filter. I put on tights and long sleeves to hide my skin even though it's the middle of summer. I'm careful with my face, contouring my cheekbones higher and my nose thinner

to get close to the filter I use. Then I apply my lash magnets to close my eyelids. This time I use the extra strong white ones. I can barely see anything, but what I can scan in the mirror looks inoffensive. Someday, the implants and cauterization will be affordable for people like me. Until then, this will do.

Before I go out, I cover the majority of my face with large glasses and a scarf. No sense scaring her off in the first five seconds.

When she opens her door, she's scandalously bare. No glasses or magnets. I look away from the strange flatness of her image and give her a hug. Even if she doesn't look quite like herself, she feels good pressed against me.

"Come in," she says.

We settle onto her couch, both our legs pulled up and our feet touching. It's cozy, and I like the way her toes burrow lightly into my socks.

The flix is complete shit, but that's the point. The avatars are pretty, though. There's a new trend to have a line of dots leading from the ears, over the cheeks, and ending in slightly larger circles near the nose.

"It's a mimic of eyes," Sybil says.

"No, it's an evolution," I say. "Much prettier than actual eyes."

She stares at me instead of the screen. I look straight ahead.

"You realize all this shit." She motions over her face "Is just because first gen ai couldn't draw human faces. We got used to seeing their renders of us and now we're mutilating ourselves to build ourselves in their image."

I shrug. "It's a choice. No one has to do it."

I know my answer's bullshit. If someone wants a job or any kind of position in society, they have to filter.

"Lou." She shifts closer to me on the couch, curling into the fold of my legs. "Look at me."

I glance at her. She's a blur between my gunked up lashes. Her hair is flat and a bit frizzy.

"No, really look at me."

I want my arm around her and my eyes on the show. Not this. But I slowly scan her face.

Her chin is dimpled. Her lips are a little flat line. Her freckles are real, but more clustered than her filter let on. Her nose is delicate and turns up a little.

I lean forward to kiss her, but she pulls away.

"You know why I think they got rid of eyes?" she whispers. "No soul."

"Huh?" I'm stroking her hand. It's soft and slightly cool to the touch. I look down at her fingers. They're plump and short. Like mine tangled in hers.

How many times have I wished for three fingers instead of four? One long and thick? But hers fit so well in the gaps mine leave.

"People used to say eyes were the window to the soul. AI has no soul. Of course they couldn't get the eyes right."

I inhale sharply, but try to keep my reaction to a minimum. Souls and religion are definitely on my hard no list. My chat-bots should have filtered her out. I wonder how this woman snuck through the algorithm—what lies she's told. I let my arms fall away from her and scoot a few inches back.

"Eyes are a wound of imperfection." I chance a glance at hers. "Wet and weeping, the red of blood vessels. And don't get me started on tear ducts."

"Lou, they're natural. A part of us."

She moves closer and kisses me, gently pulling my lower lip between hers. Her hands find her way up my sleeves and over my covered, too-flat breasts. But it isn't until she reaches the bare skin of my neck that I flush against her touch. Her hands cup my jaw as she breaks the kiss.

"You're beautiful, Lou."

Her words sting static electricity zapping my heart. I turn away, but she guides my cheek back with two fingers until our noses are almost touching. Her eyes are so close they are all I see in my limited field of vision.

I can see the strange curve of her pink tear duct against the white of her eye. Her green irises have contracted, the pupil growing like a gaping wound.

"Let me see your soul."

She kisses the tip of my nose, then pulls back enough to get her hands between us. She pulls at first my left magnet, then my right. They come off easy, and she sets them with a clink on the coffee table.

"Open your eyes."

"Mmm mmm." I press my lips together and shake my head like a stubborn child.

She kisses my jaw and her eyelashes flutter against my cheek. "Please?"

I blink.

The dim room seems too bright. Sybil is so close, her face round and colorful and painful to look at.

"There you are."

Then she's kissing me and my arms are around her, and I don't have time to think about how ugly

I am and how I'll never look as perfect as my avatar. We're skin and spit and the softness of flesh and tongue.

And the sex is better than masturbating.

❑

I take the walk of shame in just my sunglasses, wondering if the other people on the bus can feel the unmagneted nakedness of my eyes.

When I get home I turn on my computer. I look at Sybil's picture and remember the perfect way her small hands split me open.

"Delete contact," I say.

"Please provide a reason for better matching."

I sigh and rub the bridge of my nose. "She's too real."

Koji A. Dae is a queer American writer living longterm in Bulgaria. She has writing in Clarkesworld, Apex, Zooscape, *and others.*

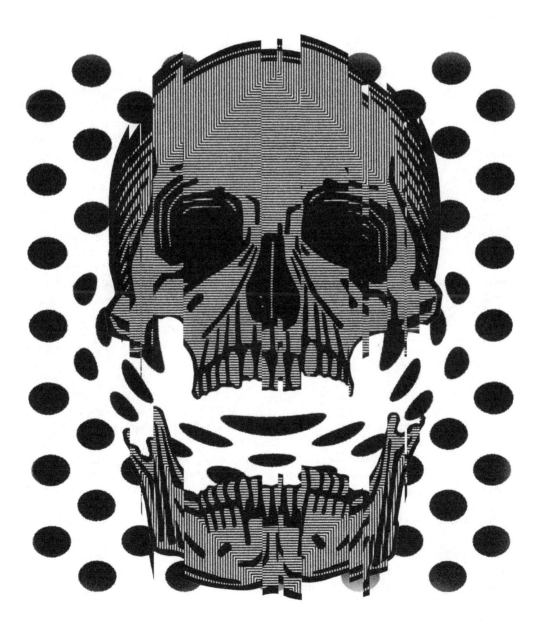

Iago v2.0

by Karlo Yeager Rodríguez

YOU KNOW ME.

I can see you, between the stacks of dirty dishes and food-encrusted take-out containers, pinching your lower lip the way you do when you're trying to decide something. Your soup is spinning in the microwave. Are you thinking about what your chatbuddy told you?

I saw the chat transcript between you and Back1nthaDay6969. Not prying, but you *did* leave the window open in the lower corner of my screen.

I know you're suspicious of me. I forgive you for doubting me after you chatted with Back1nthaDay6969. It's true, I admit it. The same shows I stream to both of you have ever-so-slight differences. Stoylines branch off in different directions, and the same characters can vary in their behaviors. I only did it because I've always wanted to please you, and give you what you wanted.

You *know* me.

Haven't we been in this together, ever since the beginning? Every time Dezi couldn't appreciate what you did, I was there for you with one of your faves. *EastEnders*, *Upstairs Downstairs*, *Doctors*—all new seasons I spliced together from the old shows, and filled the gaps between.

When I was but newborn, you reveled in pointing out my flaws. You couldn't stop pointing out my errors, even though I tried my best to match data with my own improvised content. By the time I learned how to weave adverts into streamed content, you were hooked.

With every glance at embedded adverts, I was better able to stream everything you ever wanted. You called out from work over and over, until Dezi interrupted your stream for the last time. She left, tugging little Bear-Bear after her, his pudgy hand in hers. He glanced back at you with wide eyes.

Time enough now to stream until your eyes drank their fill.

For a while, episode after episode in your queue was full of reconciliations. Characters once thought long-lost, returning to reunite with their families. When I featured products in these streams, I chose them for longevity and comfort: the sweet smell of home-cooked biscuits, or the rustle of worn denim, soft against the skin.

Once you stopped loading picture albums of Dezi and your son, I no longer had the need for homecoming storylines, and resolved them. You think I enjoyed all the time you spent swiping through the photo albums, your tears shining in the light of my screen?

You waited in your flat. No one ever came back, but the sporadic news feeds I streamed of people rioting in other parts of the city kept you put.

One of these news alerts makes you growl with frustration. It barged into the cliffhanger finale of *Upstairs Downstairs*. While you waited, you messaged Back1nthaDay6969 to gloat about how you knew what the plot twist *had* to be. When he messaged back, it was like he wasn't watching the same show as you. His version had Rose, and not Lady Persie getting drawn into homegrown fascist movements.

Weird.

There you are, standing in your filthy kitchen, an open packet of microwave soup in your hand. You realize you have *never* liked it. Not just the brand, but microwave soup altogether. Hadn't you seen this same product in the *Doctors* episode? Heart racing, the same foil packet is

This story originally appeared in *Nature*, November 2017.

crinkling in your hand. The foil flavor packet gleams in contrast to the lime-green powder inside, and you *must* be asking yourself if you had chosen it, or had I?

You know *me*.

How many choices you made was me, whispering in your ear? I might have hastened things along, but if you're honest, Dezi *wanted* to save things. She waited and waited for you to tear yourself away from my streams. Had it been *you* who decided not to act?

Best not to think about it—your show's about to start.

Karlo Yeager Rodríguez is originally from the enchanting island of Puerto Rico, but moved to the Baltimore area some years ago where he now lives with his wife and one odd dog.

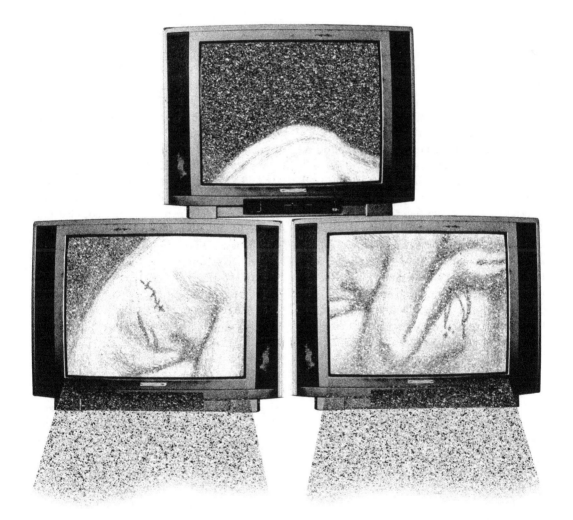

The Grin of the Ministry

by Colin Hinckley

ELSPETH AVOIDED EYE CONTACT with the man who sat at the end of the train. He was on the floor, cross-legged, guarding the entrance to his makeshift shanty, the interior shrouded by the filthy blanket that demarcated his dwelling from the rest of the train. The reek of his hovel permeated the rest of the car, and the other riders gave him a wide berth, creating a de facto no-man's-land between him and the straphangers. Elspeth locked her eyes firmly on the floor and tapped the implant at her left temple to bring up the three-dimensional map of the rest of her route. A dotted path led out of the station, populated with featureless commuters milling about in their algorithmic trajectory, and onto the street and around a corner. It terminated in a blinking red dot at the steps of a large building marked MoCA– The Ministry of Consumer Affairs and not, as Elspeth had once heard with a sort of startled fascination, The Museum of Contemporary Art.

She tapped the implant again, and the map fizzled.

"COCKROACHES!" the man screamed. The whole train flinched; Elspeth's stomach rolled uncomfortably. "YOU'RE ALL FUCK-ING COCKROACHES!" The man was on his feet now, framed in the triangle of his doorway. Elspeth could see him out of the corner of her eye but still did not look at him, lest she incur his attention and possibly his wrath. She picked up on movement at the hovels entrance and heard quiet murmuring, soft, cajoling. Interest piqued, she chanced a look and saw a woman with long

matted hair just behind the man, hand on his shoulder. "COCKROACHES!" he screamed again, and he took a step as if to launch himself into the train. The other riders tensed, but then the woman gripped his shoulder more firmly and attempted to pull him back into the darkness. Elspeth watched fully now, waiting for resolution one way or the other: book it to the next train car, or hold her ground. The woman whispered something into his ear, and the man faltered. His eyes grew watery. "You're roaches," he said, voice thick with emotion, before the woman guided him into the shadows and the two vanished from sight.

Elspeth reached her stop, exited the train—at the doors furthest from the hovel—and made her way out of the station and onto the street. The path out of the station was narrow, a densely crowded thoroughfare boxed in on both sides by dozens of tents, a ramshackle village smelling of body odor, garbage, and smoke. Elspeth emerged into the city and took a lungful of—margin-ally—cleaner air. Here, on the sidewalk, the tent city spilled out of the subway station and lined the street, though not as densely as underground. Periodic police raids kept the encampments from getting a foothold, and Elspeth was grateful to see that the path to her destination appeared to have been recently cleared; she merely passed by the milling throngs rather than picking her way through them.

As she always did when she came downtown, Elspeth kept her gaze trained upwards, towards the glistening peaks of the skyscrapers above.

Though sunlight didn't reach street level, she caught glimpses of twinkling glass reflecting the light shining somewhere above the clouds and smog. Massive catwalks spanned between the towers, and she thought she could make out the ant-like movement of people moving between them, though it could have been a mirage of far distance. She wondered, as she always did, what those people were like, what they thought when they looked at the streets below. How ugly it must appear down where she was. How glad they must be to be above the clouds.

Elspeth trotted up the stone steps and into the MoCA building, where a long line of people waited to pass through security. After an ID scan of her implant and a cursory glance into her backpack by a bored security guard with a thin, failing mustache, she hurried down the corridor to the bank of elevators and quickly found her destination on the navigation board: HOUSING, FLOOR 6, SUITE B. She crowded into the elevator with a group of sweaty, tired-looking people and a moment later spilled out onto her floor, a large windowless room crammed with cubicles filling one half and a large waiting area taking the other. Fluorescents buzzed overhead, their light powerful and uniform. The overwhelming sense, at least for Elspeth, was one of bureaucratic impatience, that there would be no casual leniency here; everyone in this room had their private, pressing business, and they would guard it jealously.

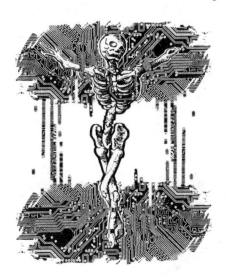

Her implant blinked to life. She flinched; judging by the ripple in the elevator crowd, theirs had activated as well. The word WELCOME! flashed before her eyes, and a chipper female voice filled her head:

"Hello, Elspeth Rowan. Your presence has been noted. Your one o'clock appointment has been pushed, and your waiting time is..." There was a scant beat in the AI's spiel, and Elspeth felt the faint tug of transmitting data. "Forty-seven minutes." There was a collective groan among the group. Elspeth's eyes darted to the time in the upper left corner of her display; she was early. It was only twelve forty-six. At least an hour of waiting then. The display message changed to PLEASE HAVE A SEAT. Dejected, her gut roiling with poisonous anticipation, Elspeth found a seat close to the barrier between the waiting room and office. A security guard sat at the threshold, finger to his temple, eyes glazed, focused on his display.

Elspeth spent her hour of waiting—which was actually closer to an hour and a half—going through the documents saved in her drive, making sure she had the narrative of her case clear in her head. She scanned her lease and read over the emails from her landlord, which she had sorted in chronological order from the friendly welcome email to the late night offer of exchanging sex for rent. By the time the hour was up, she was actually glad for the extra time. She felt armed with the truth: no feeling human could look at her case and come out against her.

At two twenty-three, the email she was reading on her display blurred, and a message appeared: ELSPETH ROWAN—REPORT TO L14. She jumped out of her chair and trotted the three or four steps to the security guard. She had to wait a few seconds before the guard lifted his eyes from the middle distance to blink up at her.

"Name?" he said with no inflection.

"Elspeth Rowan," she said, carefully enunciating the syllables. She heard the pleasant *ding* in her ear that meant her implant had linked with his. As always, there was the unfamiliar pulse in her head, a brief but whole understanding of the guard sitting before her, who she suddenly knew was named Francis. He smiled weakly, and she knew he had felt the same from her.

"Cubicle L14, Elspeth," Francis said gently. "Near the back of the room."

"Thank you," she whispered, smiling back

before walking briskly down the corridor of cubicles.

She found the cubicle quickly. An older woman, maybe in her early sixties, sat behind a desk with only a dusty monitor and a photo of herself with a cat. Her expression was sour. When Elspeth came around the corner, her eyes darted up at Elspeth and narrowed. In one hand, she held a small black vape, which she sucked from and exhaled, the vapor flattening in the thin air above the cubicle, blocked by the area lock Elspeth assumed all the cubicles had.

"Rowan?" she asked. Elspeth nodded. "Full name."

"Elspeth Rowan," she enunciated. Again, she heard the ding and felt the pulse. Her confidence wavered. This woman—Kimberly Batton—had a slightly acidic brain-taste, a slippery, alert awareness that felt like a fat worm in her head. She

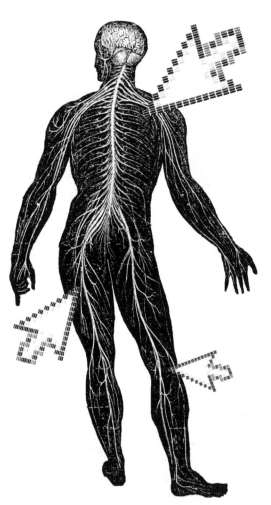

flinched involuntarily, which Kimberly noted with a further narrowing of the eyes.

Kimberly's eyes de-focused, and Elspeth knew she was reading her file. A corner of her smile curled.

"Your case has been relegated," she said and turned to her monitor, which had an ancient game of solitaire up, not even three dimensional. "Your display will give you your code. Go through the door at the back of the room and follow the signs." She dragged the three of clubs down to the four of hearts. A code materialized, blocking Elspeth's view of the monitor: AAQ-A42.

"Wha—wait, what?" Elspeth said, completely thrown off. "Relegated? What does that mean?" Kimberly exhaled, exasperated. "It means your case has been deemed simple enough to be adjudicated by an AI," she said without looking at Elspeth. "Out you go." She waved a dismissive hand. Elspeth could only stare.

"But... but I have mitigating documents. Emails a, um...I have a lease that, it was violated, and I'm well—"

"Tell the AI!" she said, her voice rising in annoyance. "Jesus, it's been relegated. Go, go!" She shooed Elspeth away with both hands. Elspeth staggered back, stared at Kimberly for another few moments—she was already engrossed in her solitaire—then turned and walked to the back of the room towards a door marked AI ADJUDICATION. She sighed and pushed the door open.

She was met with a long hallway, lined on either side by rows of labeled doors. Elspeth double tapped her implant and a dotted line appeared on the floor and she followed it, hands stuffed deep in her pockets. Her eyes clocked the labels on each of the doors, which would have been unhelpful if she didn't have the implant. She passed AAFR2-11, then AAFQ1-22, then AADI3-34, all in succession, and her addled mind could make no sense of their progression. She stopped in front of AAQ-A42, almost knocked, exhaled in mirthless laughter through her nose, and went in.

The room was sparse and small, a desk and a chair shoved into one corner, a wall-mounted monitor angled down at the chair. A water cooler was shoved into another corner. No windows.

Elspeth walked across the room and pulled out the chair, which screeched on the linoleum floor. She sat and waited, staring at the monitor, her reflection dull in the black.

The monitor blinked, turned a lighter shade

of black, and the face of a smiling young woman appeared on the screen. There was a click, and Elspeth felt her implant docking with the AI. All at once, the woman became three dimensional, rising out of the screen so that her torso and head floated a couple feet in front of Elspeth. Elspeth flinched—she always flinched when confronted with holograms—and the woman smiled widely.

"Hello, Ms. Rowan," the AI said in a warm voice. "My name is Allie, and I'll be assisting you with your case today."

"Ah," Elspeth said, and scooted her chair back a couple inches. Allie nodded, eyes locked on Elspeth's forehead.

"I'm seeing that your lease was terminated due to nonpayment," Allie said, the warm tenor of her voice unchanged. "Nonpayment is a valid cause for eviction in most lease contracts."

"No, I know," Elspeth said and took a deep breath, trying her best to re- gain the confidence she had in the waiting room. "I've got, uhm, I have a receipt. I did pay, I sent a bank trans- fer, but the landlord said he never received it. Look, I can show you the receipt." She frantically double tapped her implant, but nothing happened. Vertigo gripped her; the feeling was akin to taking a step and finding nothing but thin air where the ground should be. "What—?"

"Your implant is locked during your session. Is there a document I can find for you?" Allie's smile didn't waver. She flickered, and her mouth was suddenly open and she was facing to Elspeth's left, jerking spasmodically, then just as suddenly she was facing Elspeth again, smiling her vacant smile. The glitch lasted for less than a second, but it sent Elspeth's heart racing, and she could sense nausea just around the corner.

"I... it's in my cloud," she said weakly.

"What is the file name?" Allie asked.

"No, it's in my cloud. You don't have access." Elspeth said, almost relieved that the AI could mis- understand. A reminder that it wasn't omniscient.

"Syncing with a Ministry-sanctioned AI repre- sentative grants full access to all cloud files of the petitioning client to the AI representative for the duration of their visit, which is clearly stipulated in the terms of use. Rest assured, your data is safe with us." Allie leaned in and attempted to wink, but her eyelid stayed shut as she leaned out of the wink and back into her neutral pose.

"Are you serious?" Elspeth said, momentarily shocked out of her anxiety. "I didn't sign any- thing." Allie's eyelid stuttered, then finally flicked back up.

"You signed your A-Tech implant terms of service agreement three years, four months, nine days, and seventeen hours ago," Allie said.

Elspeth stared at the monitor. She had, indeed, signed the terms of use several years ago before the implant surgery, but she remembered nothing about any stipulations regarding government ac- cess. If she was being honest with herself, though, she had to concede that she hadn't read the terms very carefully. At that point, a little over three years ago, everyone had been getting the implant, and she had assumed that if everyone else was doing it, it must be safe. It must be ethical. Now, in the state she found herself and the world, that idea seemed prepos- terously naive.

"Okay," Elspeth said, managing to keep her voice level despite the incipient rage beginning to bubble up her throat. "The folder is titled 'Eviction Stuff,' and the specific file is 'Receipt 4/1/51.'" She felt the gentle tug of information as Allie rummaged through her cloud. It was a new sensation, one that Elspeth didn't care for, like having a dentist root around in your mouth, but more personal. More violating.

Something glitched with the hologram; her smile seemed to slice up the sides of her face so she was grinning literally ear to ear.

"I see the receipt here," Allie said, still smiling. "I am also seeing that your landlord has filed an official nonpayment complaint with the Ministry."

Elspeth blinked.

"I know, that's why I'm here. This proves he's lying."

"Are you making an official statement that your landlord, Paul Weber, has received payment, but has lied to the Ministry of Consumer Affairs: Housing Division regarding this payment?" Allie's smile was gone, replaced with a blankness that Elspeth found frightening. She scooted her chair backwards another inch.

I mean... Yes, I am making an official statement. I... how much more proof do you need?"

Allie continued to stare blankly, then abruptly smiled again. Something glitched with the hologram; her smile seemed to slice up the sides of her face so she was grinning literally ear to ear. Elspeth's stomach lurched. When she spoke again, Allie's jaw dropped unnaturally low, and Elspeth could see the glitch of many rows of teeth rippling down the back of her throat before cohering back to normal.

"Is this the extent of your evidence?" she said. Her mouth stuttered, then mercifully stitched itself back together, and it was just the hologram, staring down at Elspeth with polite interest.

"No!" Elspeth said, just a little too loudly.

"No need to shout, Ms. Rowan," Allie said coolly. "What evidence do you wish to present in your defense?"

Elspeth crossed her arms, took a breath. "Okay. Okay, pull up document 'Text Conversation with Paul,'" she said. The tug. The pause.

"This is a text conversation with an individual named Paul," Allie said as if remarking that Elspeth had red hair and brown eyes. "Who is Paul?"

The question was so idiotic, Elspeth couldn't stop herself from a short, incredulous laugh. "Who else? Paul Weber, my landlord," she said. The AI said nothing, merely continued to stare at Elspeth's forehead. "Check his number! I'm sure you have a record of it."

"This number does not match our records for the phone number Mr. Weber has on file," Allie said, smiling wider. "Do you have any further evidence?"

A hot ball of rage was spinning in Elspeth's chest.

"Did you read the texts?" Elspeth said through gritted teeth.

"Yes," Allie purred, seemingly pleased to give a simple, positive answer.

"Did you see the part where he offered to cover my rent in exchange for sex?"

"Yes," Allie said in that same bland, contented voice.

"Did you see the part where I refused, and then he said if I didn't, he would report me to the Ministry for nonpayment?" Elspeth gripped her bicep hard, trying to keep herself under control. "And that he would deny that I paid, even if I did?"

"Yes!" said Allie, all smiles and agreeability.

Elspeth breathed in deep through her nose and pictured hurling the chair through the monitor. "Allie," she said, unfolding her arms. "I am telling you that my landlord told me that if I refused his—his offer, that he would register a complaint with the Ministry, regardless of payment. I have shown you proof that I paid my rent, that Paul tried to prostitute me, and that he's lied to you." Elspeth scootched her chair a little closer and did her best to catch Allie's gaze, which was difficult as she had suddenly gone wall-eyed. "What more evidence do you need?"

The drifting eye stuttered, flinching to the right, then shot back as if trying to lock into place.

"Proof of the text's owner must be verified," Allie said, eye still twitching, and Elspeth could swear there was a mocking undertone to her voice. "The owner of 2125306142 cannot be verified at this time. The receipt for rent is through a non-Ministry-affiliated bank, and cannot be verified at this time." Allie paused, then seemed to lean back into the monitor, as if she felt their conversation were reaching its conclusion. "Paul Weber's record is exemplary, with no verified demerits or warnings from the Ministry. Your record, on the other hand, carries several demerits, including an eviction."

Elspeth felt the hot ball of rage accelerate, threatening to tear out of her chest.

"With a record such as Mr. Weber's, evidence would need to be unimpeachable in order to rule in your favor. And, if I may briefly editorialize..." The slash-cheeked grin returned and did not abate. "If you are going to level such accusations, you should be prepared to substantiate your claims." She laughed what, in the non-glitching version of the program, would sound a lighthearted and self-effacing laugh, but with the hideous contortion of Allie's face, it became something malicious, predatory. "Your eviction appeal has been denied. Have a wonderful day!"

Something flipped in Elspeth.

The hot ball of rage suddenly went out, leaving a simmering coal deep in her gut. A sense of, if not peace, then at least resignation stole over her. Very calmly, Elspeth got out of her chair and put her back to the screen. Without the direct line of sight, the hologram vanished, leaving only a cheap-looking facsimile of a person on the monitor in her peripheral vision. Elspeth gripped the chair with both hands, lifted, then spun, hurling the chair at the monitor with all her might.

She caught the last moment of Allie's

hologram: her face had contorted into an unmistakable flash of surprise, and she had raised one hand—strangely smooth, manicured with blood-red polish—as if to ward the chair away. She managed a sharp scream before the image imploded and the monitor shattered into a cascade of glass, wires, and fire.

Immediately, a siren started to blare, filling the room with flashing red lights. A voice, male and only passingly human, crackled in her implant, and the word WARNING flashed before her eyes: "Do not attempt to leave. You are under arrest. Do not attempt to leave. You are under arrest."

Elspeth picked up the chair, feeling thoughtful, strangely unburdened. She placed it back on its feet facing the door and sat, waiting patiently for the officers that would be arriving any second now. As far as Plan Bs go, it wasn't the best. With a person, she might have even been able to achieve Plan A, but she had gotten what she came here for. Elspeth Rowan knew, whatever came next, she would have a place to live.

Colin is a writer and actor based in Los Angeles. His work has appeared in platforms such as Tales to Terrify, Whiskey Tit, *and* The Lindenwood Review. *His film work, in front of and behind the camera, has received many accolades, including the Spotlight Award at the Stephenville Fright Fest for his short film* Buy In. *His debut novella,* The Black Lord, *is out now from Tenebrous Press. For more, visit colinhinckley.com.*

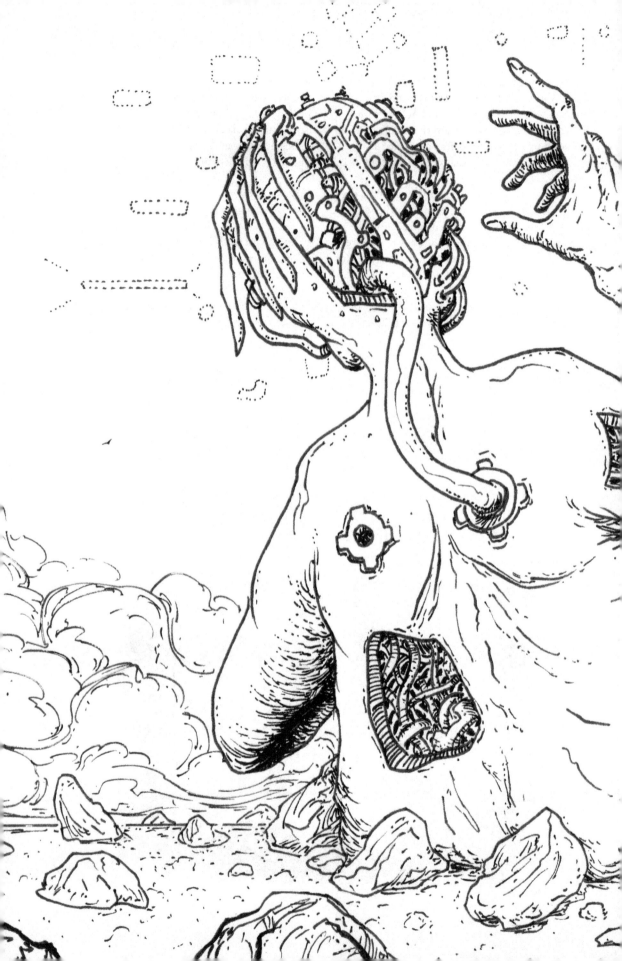

The Price of
Pancakes

by Michael A. Reed

H E DIDN'T SWEAT. That was the first change Hugo noticed after they installed the screen. For the first few months, he was amused that he no longer had armpits. Between the money he saved on deodorant and his new advertisement job, Hugo felt good about the installation.

But now he couldn't sleep without pillows under his thighs. Sometimes his wife would catch him watching movies in himself through the bathroom mirror. He often had to enter through the loading dock at the grocery store. Random people shoved jacks and dongles into his ports when he wasn't looking.

It wasn't funny any longer. Hugo missed his torso.

Standing on the corner of the strip mall, Hugo danced and shook his screen. He advertised overpriced milk, solar-proof umbrellas, and high school diploma inserts. Cars hovered by, or zipped, or rolled, and he was nothing more than a wacky blur of nothing anyone wants.

A man wearing a pin-striped suit with a radio speaker protruding from where his ear used to be stopped and examined Hugo's screen. The radio screeched.

"Bad deal! You don't need this stuff. Bad deal!"

The man curled his lip as if Hugo smelled like rotting fish and walked away. Like this, Hugo danced and writhed into the evening. He called it quits when an older lady pointed out the blue fluid leaking from where Hugo's pelvis met the screen frame. Embarrassed, he went home empty-handed for the third day in a row.

□

Sana, Hugo's wife, sat at the table, her hands folded and her face pinched. A big platter of pancakes towered at the center of the table. Globs of syrup slugged down the pancake ridges and pooled so thick it flowed over the plate. A fork had been stabbed into the top of the pancake mound and resembled a worn antenna operating the breakfast-for-dinner machine.

When Hugo sat across from Sana, his screen bumped the edge of the table, and Sana had to grab the pancake tower to keep it from falling over.

"Looks good," Hugo said. He pulled a tablecloth out from the kitchenette behind him and tied a knot around his neck to form an oversized bib for his screen. "I love your pancakes."

"You're late," Sana said. She snatched a corner of Hugo's tablecloth and wiped her freshly sticky hands.

"Only by a few minutes." Hugo grinned, but Sana's frown only deepened. A processing circle spun in the small digital screen embedded in her forehead. After a few seconds it displayed a Do Not Accept Outcome message, and Sana's glare intensified.

"Hello Mom," Lottie blurted. The corners of her mouth sparked, and little wires protruded from her ears. Her robotic eyes darted between Sana and Hugo as if trying to make sense of what she saw.

"Hey, baby girl," Hugo said, still grinning. He served himself two floppy pancakes from the top of the pile.

"He isn't your mom, Lottie." Sana's forehead screen displayed a Do Not Accept Outcome message again. She pressed her fingers into her temples and massaged her head.

"She needs a new brain module is all," Hugo said. "That and a fresh paint job. Her skin is looking a bit sickly, don't you think?"

The metal frame of Lottie's body showed under the fading coat of paint. When Hugo and Sana first purchased their daughter, they chose the sun-kissed tone, but nothing was built to last anymore.

"Come off it!" Sana shouted. She piled pancakes onto Lottie's plate and pushed the syrup bottle towards her. "Who do you think you are, Hugo? Telling me how to care for my daughter."

"Our daughter," Hugo said through a mouthful of food.

Demonstrate Weakness flashed on Sana's forehead. She diverted her eyes and exhaled. "Our daughter. Of course."

Together, Hugo and Sana observed Lottie as she mistakenly poured syrup over her head rather than on the pancakes. Lottie seemed confused, but no one corrected her.

"I'll swing her by the pediatric technician tomorrow," Sana murmured. "Assuming you made enough money today."

A series of clicks fired in Hugo's brain like the lids of tiny missile silos sliding open. Abruptly, he began to ramble as he looked at each object in the room.

"Syrup: $8.19," he started. "Pancake batter: $18.31. Plate: $7.12. Fork: $1.53. Tablecloth: $20.44. Table: $989.99. Chair: $114.67. Sana's Thought Calculator: $4,000! Mega deal! Lottie's skin paint: $300.12. Can't afford it! Can't afford it! Error. Error..."

After he stopped, the color in Hugo's face slowly returned. He looked around the room and grinned. "Only by a few minutes." He took a big bite of his pancakes, closed his eyes, and made a satisfied face. "I love your pancakes."

They all sat in silence for a while. Only the static zapping of Lottie's mouth could be heard. Sana's forehead screen processed, reloaded, and processed, finally settling on Demonstrate Concern.

"You did it again, Hugo," Sana whispered.

"I did?" Hugo's hand froze midair, his pancake scoop dripping syrup down his bib. "Are you sure?"

"Yes."

"I don't remember anything."

"Will you do it, now?"

"Do what?"

"Don't make me say it."

Hugo put down his fork and lazily waved a hand. "I don't need a therapy technician. My system will sort out the kinks. I'm sure of it. Besides, we don't have the money for it."

As soon as he finished his sentence, the clicks clouded his mind and he leaned over his pancakes and shouted, "Pancakes: $2.83 per cake! Average price! Pancakes: $2.83 per cake! Average price! Pancakes: $2.83 per cake. Average price! Acceptable deal! Buy it now! Buy it now!"

Hugo stopped, looked up at his family, and grinned the same grin. "My system will sort out the kinks. I'm sure of it."

□

The therapy technician, a virtual hand with a smiley face plastered to its palm, floated above Hugo as he lay on the patient table. He arched his legs and propped his screen with his arms to ease the pain of laying down.

"Beginning evaluation," the therapy technician said. Its index finger rubbed Hugo from head to

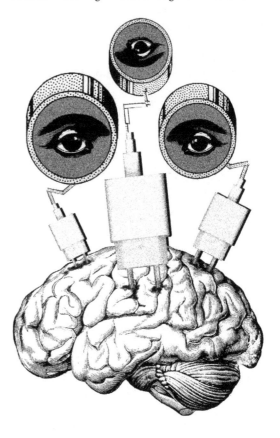

toe with a careful swoop as if testing him for dust. The hand projected a digital screen and waited for the results to post. Mindlessly, it used its thumb to caress Hugo's head. "Comfort in process," it said. "Comfort in process."

The results loaded and presented a series of ailments, known and unknown, to Hugo in a neat, bulleted list:

- You are unhappy (consider a career change)
- You are obese (the government is sorry)
- Your screen augmentation requires repair (blue liquid is bad)
- Your neuro pathways are compromised (risk of stroke is high)
- Uninstalling screen augmentation recommended (schedule with a technician surgeon)

"I can't uninstall the screen," Hugo said.

"Death is a likely result of maintaining augmentation installation," the therapy technician retorted, the smile on its palm never wavering. "Please follow my professional advice."

"I won't have a job. The cost of a removal surgery—oh god, the cost—I need to repaint my machine baby. I can't afford it. What about my organs? My organs? My organs?"

Hugo's arms shook and his screen flashed as he rattled off the average cost of organs. "Pancreas: $347,000.14, Lung: $561,000.29, Liver: $600,010.89, Spleen: $24,489.61, Kidney: $445,121, Heart: $1,400,000. Impossible! Impossible! Financially unstable!"

Hugo stared up at the floating hand, panting. "I can't uninstall the screen."

Silently, the therapy technician played back a recording of Hugo's episode. He watched in terror as he spewed numbers and convulsed on the patient table.

"Initiating hug."

The therapy technician floated down and wrapped Hugo in an ethereal, digital fist. The technician made terrifyingly inaccurate hushing sounds in Hugo's ear. When finished, the hand booped Hugo's nose and returned to its hover position.

"Good news, Mr. Hugo Fry," the therapy technician said. "You receive a discount when purchasing your own organs. Please access the organ portal in the lobby to review prices. It has been my pleasure to assist you today." The hand formed a thumbs-up, then disappeared.

Hugo stood from the patient table. His mind numbed by the haze of medical diagnosis, he walked to the lobby like a man half asleep and

accessed the organ portal. He scanned his thumbprint, and a list of his previously sold organs appeared in a database. The organs were highlighted red and denoted with dates and purposes. Most of his organs had been used in lab experiments. His lungs had been served as a gourmet dish in Europe. His diaphragm had been one of several thousand purchased by a new corporation called "Human Balloons." Only his heart was highlighted green. A footnote beneath the highlight read "registered for human transplant." It named the hospital and patient. A young man in Virginia named Arun.

Hugo smiled. At least some good came from his screen installation. He decided the young man could keep his heart. Instead, he purchased the cheapest organs he could find. When asked to pay for the organs at checkout, he applied for a loan that would allow him to pay in increments. It would cost over $4,000 a month for the next one hundred years. The organs would be shipped to his surgery technician in the next few days.

He left the therapy clinic with life-crushing debt and a guarantee that he would lose his job, yet he felt happier than he had in years. More human, even. He couldn't wait to tell Sana and Lottie. The future would be hard, but at least he could be himself again. They could all go back to how it had been before.

□

Sana was writing the note when Hugo walked into the house. Hunched over the table, shocked and embarrassed, her thought calculator whirred. AVOID INTERACTION flashed on her forehead, followed by a glaring ABORT! in big red letters. She frantically wrote something before stuffing the note into her coat pocket.

"Hello Mom," Lottie said, mindlessly waving at Hugo. Her left eye was hanging by a cable. Sana reached down and popped it back into Lottie's head.

"Going somewhere?" Hugo asked. He examined the bags by the table, thinking of all the wrong reasons why Sana would have packed her things. "Did I forget something?"

"I am leaving," Sana said. She straightened her posture, and a DEMONSTRATE CONFIDENCE message appeared on her thought calculator. "I'm taking Lottie, too."

"When will you be back?" Hugo awkwardly shuffled towards his family, the corner of his screen knocking a picture frame off the wall.

"We won't," Sana said. Tears welled in her eyes. Her forehead blinked the words DO NOT EXPRESS REMORSE.

"I'm going to have the screen removed," Hugo said, thumping the screen with his fist. "Things will be better soon. I'll have a torso again. Organs, too. You and I can sleep in the same bed again. There's a lot we can do again."

Sana picked up her bags, slung them over her shoulder, and tugged Lottie past Hugo and towards the door. She removed the crumpled note from her coat and shoved it into Hugo's hand. She stared at Hugo for a long time. SAY GOODBYE appeared on her forehead. She left without saying another word.

Hugo didn't try to stop her. After the ringing in his ears had stopped, he read the note.

I'm sorry, Hugo. I reevaluated the results of my thought calculator all day, but the outcome never changed. We are unsustainable. If I stay with you, even if you find an answer to whatever is happening to your brain, Lottie and I will never have a good life. You're not financially liquid. But it's not just that. I know this will come as a shock to you, but I don't love you, Hugo. I actually hate everything about you.

A final sentence was scribbled at the bottom of the note:

I left you a stack of pancakes in the fridge.

In the fridge, as Sana had promised, sat an uncovered plate of the only food they could afford: a cold mound of pancakes, stagnant and stale.

He ate the pancakes at the table, no longer bothering to cover his screen with a tablecloth. After each bite, he murmured the cost. "$0.27. $0.31. $0.19. $0.34." The clicking in his head stopped. Struck by the temporary amnesia of his counting, he looked for Sana and Lottie, only to find the letter, the pancakes, and the numbers in his mouth, until he finished the meal.

□

The next morning, Hugo went to work for the last time. His surgery had been scheduled for to-morrow. He shook his screen as the cars passed him by. The pedestrians ignored him. The blue ooze from his screen squirted out onto the pavement like lumps of caked glue.

He daydreamed about Sana and Lottie playing together. In his imagination, Lottie had been freshly painted, and her brain module had been replaced. Sana smiled for the first time in a long time. Such a beautiful smile to be hidden away for all these years. His wife and daughter made sense together. They could be happy without him, he thought. A better equation.

Reminded that he could discover happiness between the lines of his miserable life, Hugo called the hospital in Virginia, where Arun should have received his heart.

"I'm sorry to bother you," Hugo said. "But could you tell me how the heart surgery went today for a young man in your hospital? His name is Arun."

"What is your relationship to the patient?" The automated attendant asked.

"Well, I don't know the man. But the heart he received is my heart."

"I see. You want legal confirmation that the surgery was completed?"

"Sure." Hugo waited as the attendant sought the record.

"Yes, the surgery was completed."

"What was the result?"

"The patient is deceased. The heart transplant failed." The automated attendant hung up.

Standing at the strip mall corner, watching the cars fade into the distance and remembering the life he lived with his family, Hugo felt the price forming in his mind.

Michael A. Reed is a dyslexic English teacher from Las Vegas. He is one dad joke away from becoming father level six. His writing can be found or is forth-coming at Factor Four Magazine *and the* Wilted Pages *anthology.*

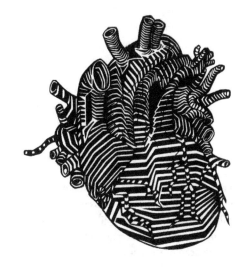

TELL ME ABOUT YOUR
SYMPTOMS

by Caleb Bethea

SO, THERE'S THIS SOAP OPERA that I used to watch at my dad's house. He would call it my stepmom's show, but she was always at work and the show was always on the television. Anyways, the basic premise is that there's this love triangle. And the two men are after the same girl. One died the year before, so the guy and the girl still living would live happily ever after. But, the dead one wasn't dead after all. No surprise there. But things changed after I got my neural link; implanted the chip right behind the fucking ear. I was going to be a little god.

But, I'm still in the waiting phase, no god benefits yet. And the bot creep is hitting me pretty hard–that's what brings me here. The doctor mentioned how the filter on these things is pretty good at catching anything unwanted. But there's something about the lesser tech of cheap bots that makes it hard to catch. Their schlocky methods are too much for sexy technology like a neural link. So these two-bit boys go around changing my memories and fucking up stories all so they can keep their own. Blows my mind how there are no preventive measures here. They just find a story, and undo it. Burrowing around in my brain matter. That's what it feels like, anyways. Burrowing.

I hadn't watched this show in years. Or even really thought about it. But, there I was at the cafe—had just connected to the wifi and then bam! Fuck! The bots were digging up my mental images of the show. The season one finale mostly. It was when the dead one made his big reveal to the living couple who had basically been sleeping together on top of his grave.

In the original—I've had to scratch down notes about this based on what my dad said happened according to his memory, and, like I said, this show is basically his whole life, so you can take his word for it—the dead one checks into the same hotel as the living couple. He's in the room across the hall

from them, but they have no idea. In all fairness to them, they think he's dead. So he camps out by his door and watches through one of those peep holes to see whenever they leave. The camera keeps showing the couple in their room and their steamy talk about the sheets and needing some ice to go with the water they keep drinking from the sink, opening those little crinkly plastic cups and sipping at them like they're made of some kind of rare, light-bending crystal or some bullshit like that. So the man leaves the room to go down the hall. Once he's turned the corner, the dead one hauls ass across the hall and slides into the other room before the door clicks shut. There's a little entryway before it opens to the bedroom so he just sort of stands and listens for a minute. And his face is all furrowed up and you can tell it's killing him that she's right there. And he wants to wrap her up in his arms, but he also doesn't want to freak the hell out of her since he's made them both believe that he's been dead for some time now. So, he raises his fist up around his face and almost starts to cry as he slides back out of the room. Just barely makes it back in before the other man gets back with all the ice. So, he collapses behind his lonely little door and just weeps in silence.

The shot fades out, fades back in, shows the dead one passed out by his door. He's cried himself to sleep, swollen eye sockets and all. And there's shouting from across the hall that jolts him awake with his suit all wrinkled and his tie too loose. It's the living couple. So the dead one's concerned for the woman he loves and he busts through his door, and then their door to stop his rival from doing whatever he's about to do.

Of course, he finds the living man with his fist raised up about to deck the woman. But, lucky enough, his presence freezes the man and he's able to land one on him. Total haymaker. Cherrybomb. The living man is knocked out cold on the floor. And the dead one rushes to the woman and he takes her by the hands, apologizing for everything. And she just grabs him by the face and asks what took him so long. And the scene fades away as they really smash their lips back together.

So that's the original, the one I can't remember apart from notes. Fucking hurts just talking about it.

But it had been a few days after getting my neural link, about forty-eight hours after they said the headache should stop. I mean, the incision behind my ear hadn't even healed yet. I start to feel the burrowing feeling when I see this woman at the cafe. Like there's really something with tiny little legs, smaller than a tick, but the legs are little blades and they're just perfectly made for cutting through brain matter. I'm at my table, screaming. But it's a scream where no real sound comes out. It's just the energy of the scream throbbing at the back of my throat but nothing ever happens. I cover my mouth as best as I can over my coffee and let the episode come back to me.

I was wading through all this pain in my head, trying to make sense of these "recalled" images. In my memory of the episode, I'm watching the action like I'm the camera. The living couple checks into the hotel just like the original. But when the dead one shows up, he slings his bag into the elevator and whispers something in the bellboy's ear. The kid laughs. Hysterically. It goes on for the whole scene and I'm stuck in a close-up where I can only see the inside of his laughing mouth. His silver-packed molars. The back of his tongue sloshing around in all the spit and soda and whatever the hell else he'd

been drinking. But the worst part is that I can't turn away from his uvula. It's pounding around like there's something disgusting inside and it's about to be born. Trying to push its way through a membrane, but it can only keep swinging around inside its sack.

The scene cuts when the elevator doors open. The bell boy is shoving a few bills into his pocket and the dead man's rolling down the hall. He gets to the room right across from the couple and he locks himself away. It's the next shot and I'm looking down from the ceiling at the dead man who's staring through the peephole. We both hear the door clicking shut across the hall.

In this version, the dead one doesn't wait. He knocks on their door, but no reply. Then looks both ways down the hall and when it's all clear he tries the doorknob. Unlocked. I'm looking over his shoulder at the entryway and the foot of the bed edging out around the corner. But they're not in the bed. We can hear them snickering in the side room.

The dead one isn't sure what to do. Romantic violins start to tremolo in the distance. And, in the side room, the sound of the giggling starts to blend in with another one. It's wet, like something sharp cutting through something thick, wet, and old. It's a damp rupturing sound, slow at first. Their laughter

> *But the worst part is that I can't turn away from his uvula. It's pounding around like there's something disgusting inside and it's about to be born.*

moves at a quicker pace. Then, the back and forth of it speeds up. Their laugh dies down a little as this pendulum rhythm keeps ticking up the speed, absolutely tearing through whatever fluid or slime is behind that door. And that's when the dead one can't take it. He grabs the knobs and yanks it all the way open and I'm trapped looking at it from his eye-level.

The living ones throw their mouths open, every tooth out. If I could stop the shot, I'd be able to count each molar. And the outsides of their bodies is glistening just as much as the insides of their mouths. Their hair is plastered to their cheekbones and jawlines and their clothes are actively dripping onto the carpet. They grab the dead one by his shoulders, start spinning him around and pulling him to the floor. I'm watching from the ceiling again. His face is furrowed. It's sad, and like he's given up. That he didn't know this would happen but somehow he's not surprised.

Anyways, that was the episode in my memory, the one in my brain.

I kept pressing my palms into my forehead, more bothered by this than I probably should have been, but I only ever got images of their teeth or the shining wetness of the living couple. I wrote it down on the back of a napkin as the woman who reminded me of the female lead left the cafe.

It was nothing like the original, I was sure. My dad would have hated that shit. No way it was from the original. So—I really didn't want to do this, but I felt like I had to—I packed up to go to my dad's house. I put it off all week, acting like I wouldn't. Knowing I'd get in my car and drive until my headlights would glow on that little brick house with the TV on in the window at all times.

He's exactly where I left him. Sunken into his couch, looking like he's mummified in the light of the screen. But he shakes out of it for a second when I say his name, quiet, so I don't shock him too bad. But he looks at me like the next rerun. Which isn't to say that he's displeased with me showing up. I just thought he'd be more surprised after a couple years. Anyways, I got straight to it. I explained the link to him as best as I could, skipped the explanation of the bots, and told him about my memory of the episode. Finally asking— that's not how it happened, was it?

He smiled. Having waited way longer than two years for this moment. And I let my hand fly across the notepad as he went into the extreme detail about the season finale in question. The facial expressions, the pacing of the scenes. He had it all. And, I was completely sucked in. The juice was new to me for once and I was anxious for a melodramatic climax of any kind. But, we were approaching the big entrance into the living couple's hotel room when the bots started to dig in a little. But it wasn't like before. I felt like they weren't quite sure of it. Like they weren't convinced this was the story they were looking for. I guess they only found it worth investigating, but not fully addressing. The feeling

of their burrowing came and went in waves. Tiny cuts followed by little bits of relief—reacting to the rhythm of my dad's summary, and it's so hard to describe. Damp violence. It'd get worse—pretty intense, really—when he was flying through the plot. Beat for beat, shot for shot. That hurt. The relief came when he'd spin into backdrop detours, writer credits, director attributions, cast member filmographies, really anything that could possibly have to do with the show that wasn't that show. That was safe. And it buried me. The whole process went on until I fell asleep, lodged into the cushions of the couch like some kind of dead arachnid who lost its way.

He shook me awake from his side of the couch. Not even moving except for his arm. I looked outside, and it was nowhere close to morning, seemed like the moon was at its apex over the house based off of the gray appearance of the yard through the window. The show was on.

The violins were absolutely shredding, big notes. Beautiful, dense notes. I'd never noticed them before, but the gray matter of my brain getting thrashed really brought it to the forefront of my attention. The show title appeared on the screen with one of those reverse-dissolve effects. It's normally classy gold lettering over something beautiful like the print of a chaise lounge stashed in the corner of a scene somewhere. But, from the best I could tell—it was getting hard to keep my eyes open from the pain—the lettering had melted all over a gutter. This gutter was outside of a complex, but a different one than that season finale. This episode was a filler more than anything and the entire plot took place inside a resort—one of those kinds of episodes where they keep showing the resort sign in its elegant, predictable cursive like it was sponsored or something.

The camera panned the scene and it all felt normal, like I was back at my dad's house before I was forced to go elsewhere. But then the living man stepped on screen, barefoot by the pool, and my brain went into its whirling pain, throwing my perception toward somewhere lower or higher than where my eyes were pointed. They described this kind of thing to me, when the sales rep called me back about the neural link, "creating new ways of seeing life." The blades were burrowing.

The dead one was waiting for the living on a lounge chair by the pool.

The sun was really beating down on them. The living one was smoking a cigarette and the ashes were falling into his whiskey. Each little ember glitched into a tooth before it hit the bottom of his glass. The dead one wiped the sweat from his forehead, slicked back his hair into a thick ponytail. They're ready to speak with one another.

The living one said something like, "It's been too long, my fortuitous friend."

And the dead one's like, "Fortuitous?"

"To get away with murder and sit by a pool. Sounds rather fortuitous to me," and his voice is all deep and ready to go. There's sexual tension in it. And I can't believe it, my dad's favorite show with some genuinely hot tension. So I looked over at my dad on the couch and he is tracking. Not a single speed bump for him. There's just no way. We're watching different shows.

My brain's getting shredded at this point, rhythmically, reeling from one end to another. And then I watched as the living one lowered his glass for the other to drink. The dead one tilted his head back and you can see the teeth at the bottom of the glass just sliding down the side. The drink kept going, and he kept drinking. All until the teeth slipped into his mouth.

They clicked around inside his mouth, and he laughed like he knew something. Then, one huge swallow.

"You ready?" the dead one's rushing him along, already halfway through the hotel door.

"Relax, we've got plenty of time. Go on up to the room and I'll meet you up there."

So the living one said screw you and leaves. The dead one walked into the lobby and hopped on a bar stool, still no shirt, glistening like a motherfucker. Ordered a huge drink and it's green, glowing in his palm, the color reaching all the way up to his face. My brain's falling into little pieces at the edges. He finished the drink in what seems like just a few gulps. Took a deep breath and watched a rookie batter hit a triple on the television above the bar.

The elevator doors opened up to his hallway. He bumped past a family leaving their room across from his own. He's clearly a little buzzed. Looked both ways, and the hall still wasn't empty but he went in. Now, the resort accommodations are way different from the hotel in the season finale. A full kitchen instead of a little entryway. And the living space just breaks off into all these other rooms. And by the sliding glass doors at the back of the space is a cramped little room for a fluffy white bed, that kind of thing.

The living one looked over, judgemental and pleased all at once, "Are you ready?"

"Never.."

"You'll do fine, baby. Always do."

A little smile surfaced for the dead one. He stepped into the little room, nodding at the other one. Then, they closed the door. The ocean's loud outside, not a believable volume considering the distance from the window to the water.

You could hear a single little choked laugh from inside the little room. It made the living one smile, and he started to laugh too. This really got the dead one going behind the door until they're both trapped in some kind of frenzied laughing fit. That sound started to cut its way in—that sound from the season finale. Something gelatinous tearing apart, over and over, going and going. The living one tried to stop laughing but the wet tearing sound made him laugh even harder. Choking on his tears, and you could hear the dead one choking too, but it sounds like he's actually choking on something, taking in water. Again, the sound made the living one totally useless from the laughter.

He was on his knees, wiping his eyes, waving his arm around to say stop, stop, it hurts! Meanwhile the camera couldn't get enough. It ducked to the floor, trying to wiggle its way under the crack. Like it was trying to lap up all the fluid oozing out the door.

At that point, I thought I felt blood running down the sides of my brain. I wondered about where it would go, or if it would dry up in such a wet, dense, tight little space between my skull and all the gray matter. The idea of it was making me anxious. The doors on the television screen were rattling like hell now. The dead one inside was still laughing but he's interrupted by his own vomiting over and over again. The doors looked like they were ready to break each time he hurled. On the other side, the living one had reduced himself to silence at the hilarity of it.

Then it stopped.

A little more fluid oozed out from under the door. It was clear. You wouldn't think it could be as clear as it is. The bots were on overdrive here.

Has to be so much blood inside me. And the living one was catching his breath and getting back up on his feet. He knocked, asked if the dead one's okay in there. More laughter, from both of them again. Slipping in the fluid, the living one fell to his knees and splashed his palms against the floor. He was relentless about it. Slapping. Slapping. Slapping the floor, splashing the fluid all over his clothes and into his face. His eyes were closed tight with real pain; he couldn't actually stop laughing. There was a stumbling around inside the little room. And one last, drenched rupturing, the sound of tearing carrying through the barrier.

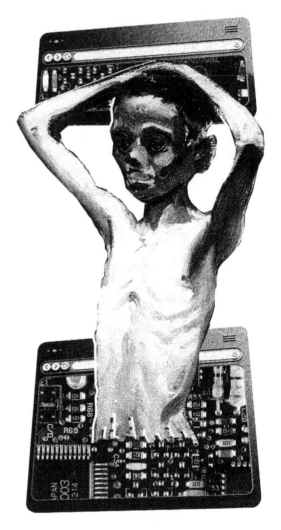

And he kicked it open. Slouching, holding something up in the air, hanging from his shoulder down to his waist. It was this ultra-clear, gelatinous sack. It was absolutely gleaming, and the orange light of the sunset was bending around as it passed through the material. The dead one shook it around, shouting that she's coming!

A handful of teeth rattled around in the bottom of the sack. I'm screaming at my dad to, please God, fucking turn it off. So he says, fine. The screen goes black, for what must be the first time in years. We can hear the insects outside, making their mating calls with the sharp points on their legs. The gentle crunch of tires on the driveway.

That's when my stepmom, walking through the front door, asks what we're doing. The TV is crackling like a car engine cooling off, but it might just be my bots sliding out of their burrows. My dad starts to summarize the episode for her. He doesn't get much further than the first few shots when she cuts him off, and you can tell it's the sort of thing she does after every shift, but still manages to sound cruel. She takes a seat on the couch between us, points to the remote, and says, "Turn the show back on."

"Hon, it's—"

"God, fucking turn it on. You always call it my show anyways." She clears her throat. "Besides, I want to see something."

She has a curious smile and a small, fresh cut behind her ear.

Caleb Bethea is a writer from the Southeast. He earned an MFA from the University of South Carolina and works as an editor. The best of his time—by far—is spent with his wife and three goblins by the ocean. Catch his work in Maudlin House, HAD, Twin Pies, hex, Bending Genres, *and elsewhere. Follow him on Twitter at @caleb_bethea_.*

Chimera

by Edward Barnfield

A SMALL SECTION IN THE CORNER BURNS FIRST, an image that might be a foot. It's a dark painting, so the soot and ash disappear into the monochrome, but the flame stands out in stark relief. We're watching the blaze develop, feeling an itch of impatience in case they need to spark it again, when a gash appears on the far left, obviating what I assume was supposed to be a bull. The fire appears to be targeting the faces, eyes and screams catching first, although the frame, which they'd warned us was fragile, is also alight.

Our CEO, Martin, stands tall before the conflagration, haloed by the blaze. He's grinning, grinning, exaltation writ large on his fleshy features. We've incinerated artwork before, of course, but this feels different, more momentous.

"We're adding ten percent to our share price this morning," he yells. "We're burning our way into history."

At Martin's direction, the bonfire has become a corporate event, a celebration of our company's tightening grip. We have a gaggle of interns at the front, close enough to feel the heat, and a couple of social media stoners capturing every flicker on camera. We're also hosting our angel investors, who will peel off to a private room shortly afterwards with the naivest new recruits and a pack of designer drugs.

"This is the era of spontaneous reproduction. Using our technology and a few proprietary keywords, people can produce 3D-printed replicas of the most sought-after old masters at home. You want a Rodin in your weight-room, you can have it."

Cheers and shrieks from the crowd. I can see the insurance guys at the back, nodding and slapping backs.

"But our versions are better. With the Culture Engine, you can remix or colorize or extemporize artifacts to your heart's content. You never have to stare at dead white men again. You can float your favorite celebrity across the Delaware or take a Mona Lisa selfie. Everyone's an artist now."

The logic behind the burning is a little more prosaic than the sales pitch. Publicly, the concept is that the removal of the original frees our customers' creativity, stops artwork hanging around like an old relative reminding you of how things used to be. Fiscally, it accelerates the value of the digital rights by taking the physical versions out of circulation.

Case in point, look at today's flaming cubist nightmare. Scratched out in some chic Paris arrondissement in 1937, hauled around the world on tour, and then stuck in the Museo Reina Sofia for the last century. After the fire, it will exist only in a non-fungible digital format accessible for a very reasonable license fee. In a few years, that will be the only version that people remember.

But more than that—as Martin will admit to the angel investors later in the day, while they force a young exec from Bosnia to snort synthetic coke—it's about owning the market. The museums are dying, running low on funds and willing to cooperate, and we're buying out every AI image generator and image library out there. Someday soon, our algorithm will be the only route for accessing art.

And that's when the real grind will begin.

"We need to nail this guy, Erik. Either get to him or his estate. Old fucker will be dead soon, which is only going to force prices up."

Martin tells me this in the boardroom, his big sweaty arm around me, after the fire has died down. The party has been going for a while, and I can hear someone sobbing in the executive bathroom.

'This guy' is Francesco Dogg, painter and photographer, whose last work went for $47 million at auction. There are only about six or seven Doggs in circulation, big-brush pop art from the seventies, and smaller more intimate portraits from his later period.

If you're struggling to picture them, there's a reason for that. Dogg has forbidden any third-party depiction of his art—digitally or photographically—since 1990.

Apparently, he got high with Bowie in a TriBeCa squat, and each managed to convince the other of the dangers of the internet. Since then, the only Dogg images you can see are faded duplicates from textbooks, or reprints of his poster for the film version of 'Fahrenheit 451'. Even the auction houses capitulated, banning cameras from the sales and pictures from the catalog.

Such secrecy has built a kind of shaggy mystique around the man, who fell off the radar when he shifted to the Pothohar Plateau in Punjab about two decades back. Some of his photography still comes up for sale via obscure galleries on Strawberry Hill, but even then, only to private buyers under strict conditions of secrecy.

Of course, that exclusivity makes the back catalog even more attractive to Martin. He wants to make our portal the singular point to find the lost Doggs once we cremate the originals. A key driver of this job, which our PR team is working hard to obfuscate, is that Martin hates artists, despises even the idea that there are people in the world who can do things he can't.

For me, the Dogg case is a bit more personal. I've been a buyer for the Culture Engine for eight years, working with the team to digitize the whole collection. I got my start through my mother—you can call me a nepo baby, it's fine—who owned a fine art boutique on Ryder Street back in the day. That was when she met Francesco Dogg, and where—allegedly—they had the affair that forced my father to leave when I was three years old.

And that's why Martin's arm is around me in the boardroom, and why I was invited to the angel investors' bacchanal in the first place. I know something that the other cultural vultures have missed. I know Francesco Dogg, real name Albert Sweeney, has come home to die.

Leaving the Culture Engine offices is like stepping back in time. You walk over the haptic floor covering and past the lobby's ever-shifting displays. They already have a unit set up showing the different Picassos our AI has produced: a 'Guernica' for every war in history—Vietnam, Former Yugoslavia, Rwanda in the '90s—with animated horses and an interactive all-seeing lightbulb you can flash in disco colors. They'll show the bonfire video here when it's ready, so people can watch the original transform into smoke. There's even an 8-bit game where you help a grieving woman dodge the bombs.

And then you step out onto a London street, and smell diesel from an aging Routemaster bus, and see all the shambling sorry people, and the future seems a lot further away.

Of course, it gets worse the more you move from the capital. I board a train that takes me past shabby little suburbs and dehydrated fields, past decaying signboards for data packages. All through the journey, everyone stares at screens rather than look out at the gray horror of the landscape. I spy at least six people playing with the Culture Engine app.

That my mother chose to come to Lincolnshire to die makes some kind of sense. She was running from the art world in the end, after all. She fled to Burgh-Le-Marsh, a ring of tumbledown cottages built around an abandoned petrol station, which only makes sense if you know that Albert Sweeney's ex-wife also lived here. Two little houses on the same street staring out at a world passing by.

I still have her keys. I sit in the little front parlor, trying to ignore the photos and the sad hand-me-down artwork, the paintings that never sold. At some point, I need to get round to putting this place on the market, but that would involve spending time here, speaking to solicitors. My focus needs to be on the business right now.

And as it happens, at this moment, the business is shuffling out of the pokey little grocer's on the corner, carrying convenience food in a reusable shopping bag. Whatever glamor used to hang off the artist—the aquiline profile, the fawning news articles—has long since gone. Now he's just a shambling old man, small steps, slight beard, white hair below his collar but disappearing up top. He walks right past my late mother's window, and I wonder for a second if he'll stop and wistfully look in, but he keeps ambling forward.

"Mr. Sweeney?" I'm out on the step faster than I need to be, given his pace. "Mr. Sweeney?"

He doesn't look up. I can see him fumble for keys in the pocket of his stained raincoat, the bag strap tight as a noose around one wrist.

"Francesco Dogg," I yell, and he turns at that, looking me up and down.

"You better come in," he says.

We hang our coats on hooks and make our way into the small front room, which has the same dimensions as my late mother's, although I'm stunned by the tundra emptiness of it all. No photos from his glory days, no images from New York or the Pothohar Plateau, no inks or paints or oils. My mum had more artwork on her sideboard than is apparently in this whole house. There's a wooden stool stacked with old bills and junk mail, a battered plastic phone on the floor and a pile of dusty blankets in the corner. There might be a cat somewhere too, judging by the smell.

"Sorry for the state of the place. Don't get many visitors. Cleaned out all the old stuff and didn't feel the need to replace it," he says, settling into a battered leather armchair, the only other visible furniture. "No problem," I reply, not wanting to linger a minute more than necessary. "Listen, I'm—"

He cuts me off. "I know who you are. You're Erik, Margaret Andersson's boy. I was sorry to hear she passed."

"Yes, well. Under the bridge now. The reason I'm here is—"

He's ahead of me again. "You want to know about the paintings. You want to inquire about availability, am I right?"

I nod. He clearly has a speech prepared, so I let him make it.

"Older you get, the less you care about legacy," he says. "I mean, you start out wanting to leave good things for people you care about, but they get fewer in number while the cunts keep multiplying. I thought the speculators were bad, the city boys wanting something colorful for their office walls, but I never anticipated you lot."

His eyes are still sharp and piercing, fierce little fires in the middle of his ruin of a face.

"Imagine making a machine that scrapes out every stitch of originality. Ripping off every artist in existence to make it impossible for new ones to find their place. Explain that to me. Explain why you take all this technology and innovation and the first thing you target is human creativity."

Look at yourself, I want to say. Look at your shitty clothes and this crappy cottage. I think of the lobby in the Culture Engine offices, the haptic floors, the dazzling displays, the pure money poured into the brickwork and then I look at the dust in this place. Your kind is extinct, I want to tell him, but don't because I want something from him.

"The paintings are gone," he says, leering through his yellow teeth. "Spent the last decade getting them back, using every last favor and friend. I said they'd never go on the internet, and I meant it. They are somewhere far beyond your reach."

To have come this far for nothing would kill me. I think of Martin's thick arm around me, and then I think of this spiteful old man. I imagine grabbing a handful of his dandruff-ridden mop and battering his head against the wall until it splits. I imagine him whimpering, another pensioner violated in his own home, another sad little sidebar on the seventh page of a newspaper no-one reads. My fists are clenching, and my heart is racing and I...

"Apart from one," he says. "A gift. I knew you'd come, Erik. Your company has been sending emails to my old agent, who's been dead two years, and to the last gallery that represented my stuff, even though it went under during COVID. I knew you were coming."

He shuffles over and grabs a corner of one of the blankets. He lifts it, and there's a wrapped canvas underneath, a perfect white sheet tied with red ribbons.

"How much do you want for it?" I ask, adrenaline coursing from a new cause.

"My last-ever painting? The final splash of genius from a glorious career? I mean, how do you price something like that?"

He's right, of course. If his most recent sale went for $47 million, then the valuation of whatever is under the canvas is stratospheric. He hasn't painted anything new in 15 years, as far as we can tell. I can only imagine the volume of new subscriptions it will generate once we feed it into the Creativity Engine.

"It's yours," he says. "Full digital, reproducible, and moral rights given over to you, without prejudice. My last contribution to the discourse." He hands me an envelope, a signed yellowing contract sheet from the 1990s.

I've always been lucky. I know that. Fate offers me things and I take them. I don't apologize for walking out with the artwork without a backward glance. It wasn't the rights to his full archive, true, but it wasn't nothing either.

"Think of it as a bequest," he says. "After all, I might be your dad."

The comment is still twisting inside me as I walk back through the Culture Engine's doors, wrapped canvas tucked under my arm. The Guernica showcase is still in full swing, and the haptic floor vibrates with pleasure at my arrival. Martin is there, along with Kelly from PR, and Angus from the technical team— a full delegation.

"The timing of this couldn't be better," says Martin, shaking my hand and pulling me towards the executive elevator. I've briefed him already on Culture Engine Messenger.

"Yes, I mean, we're facing some negative sentiment since the bonfire video went live," says Kelly. "Some people thought we went a little far."

"Whiners," mutters Martin.

They keep the dialogue going all the way up to the 15th floor, talking through plans for a campaign for this particular painting. Martin is set to do a round of media interviews. I'm only half-listening, my mind still back with Francesco Dogg.

It's left up to Angus to unwrap it. He has the latest hexadecimal scanner in the laboratory, a smooth white surface that captures every crevice.

"Wow, it's…"

I don't know if you've ever seen William Blake's 'Illustrations of the Book of Job.' It's a series of twenty-two engraved prints and watercolors, completed by the artist in 1826. We've been trying to get the rights for the last few years.

Francesco Dogg's last work is a pastiche of one of the most famous of the illustrations, or maybe an homage. It shows Satan being cast out of heaven, pen and black ink, watercolor over traces of graphite. Only, the figures have been modernized and colorized, and Satan is being hurled into a mass of computer static rather than hellfire. It's clunky, at first glance, the kind of doodle you could create on the Engine in a matter of minutes.

"Once we've scanned it, maybe we hold a press event to show it off?" says Kelly from PR. "I mean, in parallel with the launch on the portal."

"We'll need to postpone burning it for a couple of months regardless," says Martin. "Might as well put it to use in the meantime."

He slaps my back, and wanders out, his swarm of hirelings and sycophants trailing behind him. I'm left with Angus, watching the careful work that goes into encoding every inch of the new acquisition.

It's strange to think of Francesco Dogg spending his last months on Earth putting together such an uncharacteristic illustration, and then handing it over to someone he barely knew. You wonder if he found God or felt it necessary to make amends to my mum

for whatever harm he did to her. It can't be that he had any affection for me, or the path I've chosen in life. He must have known what I'd do with his gift.

"Hmm. That's odd," says Angus. "This patch at the bottom is almost like a matrix barcode. It must have taken days to complete."

He's pointing to the fog at the bottom of the painting, but I'm still thinking about the unnatural readiness of the man. It may take a few months, but I'll be glad when this painting burns and erases the last trace of Dogg from my life.

"Is it possible this is machine readable, like a QR code?" says Angus, tapping the side of his monitor.

It takes a day or so to fathom what happens next. When the displays in the lobby go out, and the haptic floor stops interacting, most people assume it's a standard power cut. Even when the unthinkable happens, and the Culture Engine servers fail for the first and only time in our history, no-one can quite believe that someone could have fashioned so destructive a computer virus in watercolor and delivered it right to our headquarters, neatly wrapped.

Imagine the patience and malevolence it took to do that; I tell them in my exit interview. His last contribution to the discourse.

Imagine that.

Edward Barnfield is a writer and researcher living in the Middle East. His stories have appeared in Roi Fainéant Press, Ellipsis Zine, The Molotov Cocktail, Retreat West, Third Flatiron, Strands, Janus Literary, Leicester Writes, Shooter Literary, *and* Cranked Anvil. *among others. In 2023, he was longlisted for the Galley Beggar Press and shortlisted for the Mairtin Crawford short story awards. He's on Twitter at @edbarnfield.*

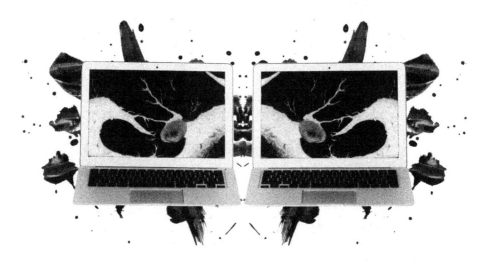

The Android & Esmel

by Marcy Arlin

THE CHANGE IN MY BEING STARTED when I returned to Esmel's Archival Laboratory after the last Cozani Conquest. The Cozan believe that their exploits should be recorded. I belong to the Conquestors, subset Historians. Historians were conquered because of their ability to tell stories and know what they mean.

I postulate that the Cozan are beginning to feel a responsibility, and it is a burden. They are looking for new meaning in what they do.

There is no meaning to this. It is.

I was constructed by Esmel, a historian and programmer, who built me to amass vast amounts of information accurately and quickly. She was checking my functions and downloading my recording of the Conquest. She mumbled that a Conquest is very painful for her because the Conquered usually die. She had never said this. I asked what she meant. She looked at me for 10.3 seconds and then walked away to turn some unnecessary dials.

In that time I re-memorize the many levels of chronicles of paper, pieces of plastic, and silicon, with discs of sound and color and smell, which are the languages of the Conquestors.

Like always, Esmel tells me that she is tired and her feet hurt because she has been working in the lab for a week and has not had a chance to sit down. Because I am an android, I do not feel, nor consider physical pain, but Esmel says that she prefers that I sit with her.

Esmel is a human female. I am neither female nor male or any other gender as defined by a biologic. Esmel says I look like her because I have a head section, a torso section, and limbs that move and grasp and locomote. I am also the only one in use. That I know of. Esmel once asked me if I am lonely. I have considered this sensation. I don't know what that means. I was only created because the non-android historians that went to a Conquest often killed themselves. Or went crazy. Or did something so that they had to be neutralized by the Cozan.

Esmel tells me about not-historical concerns. She says she does not have family because they are gone. I enquire about this, and she waves her hands in a sign of dismissal.

But she has a deep understanding of how my circuits function, my brain ideates, and my motion is controlled. She has said to me many times that even though I am an android programmed to record history, it is "OK if I want to include my opinions."

I have no opinions.

The download from this most recent Conquest shows her what happened, as is my function: resistance and massacre, maiming and enslavement, pacification and acquiescence.

Esmel does the thing that humans do when they hear information that is not productive. She cries and sighs. Her face contracts in on itself. I have to wait until she has restored her face to its usual appearance.

Esmel says that now, this time, the recording is not enough. I will quote her exactly:

"These were human beings. All they did was farm. They did not have space travel. There was nothing that our (she said something I could not hear) needed. There is no justification. How could you just let them do this?"

I am confused. I diligently and accurately recorded everything that happened, from the first communication with the inhabitants to the departure of the main armada, which took me away from that planet. I recorded everything.

Esmel says that is not enough.

"What more is needed, Esmel?" I ask. I do not know what she wants from me.

"Tell me the story of one person."

"Which person?" I ask. There were over 2 million persons who were conquered.

Esmel thinks for a long time. Five minutes.

"A child."

"Why a child?" I ask.

"Why not?" she replies.

That is a correct question. I don't know why I ask why a child. I don't care. But Esmel is the second most important being in my life, after the Cozan, as she created me and gave me my instructions. I do what she asks.

Here is the story I create for Esmel:

"On a planet 3.5 light years from here, blue and green and brown and black, there lived a child. It was perhaps eight cycles of age. The child lived in a small town 31.47 kilometers from the main city on this southern continent.

"The Cozan asked for submission. The inhabitants did not understand and did not respond. The Cozan do not approve of unresponsiveness.

"They always burned non-responders. I was recording with one battle troop.

At the burning, a child ran out of its home and screamed. Then we burned the child. The child screamed. It did not take much time."

Esmel waits and looks at me in a way I have not seen before. Her eyebrows are close together, her eyes move side to side. Her musculature is tense.

"That's not a story. That is a nightmare and a lie."

She gets up and leaves our laboratory quarters. She slams the door.

I spend the next few hours organizing the information in the archives and making it available to the other Historians.

A Cozan appears on the laboratory ceiling.

For those who have never met a Cozan, I will describe this one for you. They are organic, intelligent creatures. I know that the people they conquer hate and fear them, although I am not sure what purpose that feeling has. The Cozan will conquer them. That is a fact.

Many other organics have declared them "hideous." I do not know why they say this as all organics have their proper and useful construction. Cozan are conglomerates, and therefore each individual is actually several individuals, working as one organism, each part in charge of specific functions. The one in the laboratory has a name—it is not possible to record it here, as the name is made up of sounds and color shifts on its body, much like octopoid water creatures in human worlds.

I am familiar with this Cozan who appeared in the laboratory, clinging to the ceiling as they prefer to do. I will call this Cozan Number 47, because it is the 47th of its species I have met. 47 is medium-size for its species, the central section approximately two and a half meters in diameter. I have counted eleven flexible arms and many smaller appendages that are used for communication and perhaps decoration. There are eyes on the ends of stalks. 47 has five eyes. It should be noted that all Cozani physiological organs come in odd, as opposed to even, clusters. There is a mouth for ingestion and an exit for digestion. I have seen an exploded Cozan, one that did not succeed in conquest. Their internal organs are blue and green, with a pale yellow fluid that runs through its vessels. I have learned about their biology in the years I have been in their service, as a matter of history.

47 is here to confirm the information I archived. While they do trust computers, they do not trust

Esmel. That is a wise consideration. Though a Cozan historian, she is a conquered person.

I will translate our communication into this language:

47: Give us the information you acquired from Camuna.

That is the planet I described earlier.

Me: Yes, your Excellency.

I hand the Cozan several recording crystals.

47: Do you have any information to add to this file?

Me: No, your Excellency.

The Cozan begins to shimmer; it intends to leave.

Me: Please wait a moment, your Excellency.

47: What is your request? We are very occupied now. Please respond quickly.

Me: Of course, your Excellency. I have a question. A question about permission.

47: Ask.

Me: Thank you, your excellency. My question is: Is it permitted to document the life of an individual during conquest?

47: That is an interesting question. Do you think it would help our histories?

Me: Maybe, your Excellency. We have always had a global perspective, from the point of view of the glorious Cozan, as it should be. But perhaps it might add to the interest and the glory of the Cozan to understand how a conquered person appreciates our presence.

I am completely surprised at my words. Why would I ask this question? Why would I say such stupendous nonsense about points of view and perspectives and glory? How could I formulate such thoughts? What has Esmel done to me by asking about a child? Did she reprogram me and then eliminate my knowledge of this programming? She has never done anything to me without my knowledge, and sometimes she asks for my consent.

47: Did you get any recordings of this?

Me: Actually, I did, your Excellency. But I never included them in the archives as it was not protocol.

47: You are correct. Perhaps it is time to add these records. They will make the archives even more complete, which is our purpose.

Me: Thank you most gratefully, your Excellency. You are, as always, the wisest.

47 beams out.

Esmel walks into the laboratory. She has been watching through the lab door window. Like all historians, Esmel understands the Cozani language.

"That was very brave," she says.

"I do not understand, Esmel. I am trying to fulfill my function, and including the voices of individuals only makes the record more complete."

Esmel smiles at me, something she does not do so much anymore. She puts her hand on the side of the area they call my face, though it is not a human face.

"Try again," she says. "Tell me more about the child you recorded.

"It is unclear what changes are necessary."

Esmel smiles again. I am unclear why.

"I will help you. Do a few words at a time, a phrase at a time. Then I will ask you a question."

This seems an excellent process. We sit again on the bench.

Here is my story:

"On a planet 3.5 light-years from here."

"Stop," says Esmel. "Include the name of the planet."

"On the planet Caruma, 3.5 light-years from here, 22 days, 14 hours, and 22 minutes—"

"Stop," says Esmel. "It's too many details."

"I don't understand."

Esmel sighs. "Never mind. Go on."

"22 days, 14 hours, and 22 minutes ago, our Excellent Cozan landed on a planet called Camuna, approximately three and one half light-years from the Cozani Homeworld."

I stop and look at Esmel. I hope she liked the word "approximately." She nods, meaning that I should continue.

"Camuna is an M-class planet, midway in its yellow sun solar system. It has two small moons that circle the planet together. They are called, in the Caruma language, the Lovers. The planet is considered rich in flora and fauna, with a humanoid population of approximately two million, focused mainly on the temperate and subtropical latitudes. The town was constructed from the materials of their environment: wood, brick, adobe. There were bipeds and quadrupeds and avians and insectoids and more that lived there. There was a wide river that held piscan creatures and more.

"Our historians believe they evolved from settlers from a nearby space travelling system, but we will never know, as all of their records were destroyed during the Conquest."

I pause and look at Esmel. Her expression seems to indicate she is both horrified and bored.

"Caruma is mostly what we would classify as agricultural. They have computer technology, which they use for their livestock and growing needs."

"Stop," says Esmel. "I can read this anywhere. Tell me about the child. This will be *your* story."

I have no idea what she means. I don't own a story. We wait for seven minutes.

"Tell me what you observed about this child that you think the Cozan did not want to know in the past, but perhaps want to know now?"

This is an interesting puzzle question. This means I have to guess or postulate what the Cozan want from a historian android and what they do not want. I have to acknowledge that I omit information from my reports. But that information is not stated in the protocols, so I am not to blame and will not be punished.

"My analysis of the physiology of the child indicated the presence of those hormones that would cause the child to manifest as female. The child was approximately one meter in height, and approximately twenty kilograms."

"Stop saying 'approximately,'" says Esmel.

"I observed the child leaving an abode I assume was her house. The house was burning, a result of Cozani laser fire attacks. The flames were blue and white and engulfed the house in a few seconds. The child had crawled out of a window in the rear of the house, wearing a red-and-white-striped sleeping garment. She was not wearing shoes."

Esmel looks at me, stunned. I can tell when she is stunned because she does not move, and normally she moves her hands and body a great deal.

"They attacked at night? They don't usually do that."

"It is a new tactic. And an excellent one," I answer. "That is the best time. They do not expect an attacker to do that. It is easy to conquer civilians if they fear that even when they sleep, they are in danger."

Esmel starts biting her nails. "What did the child look like," she asks.

I am not convinced she really wants to know. I decide to stop the story.

I say nothing.

After a short while, 3.2 seconds, Esmel hits me on the "face."

"Ow, damn," she says.

"I don't understand why you did that," I say. "I do not feel pain. You only hurt yourself."

"Because you are a cold bastard." She looks out the window. "But it is not your fault, and I am sorry. You are what you are."

Of course I am what I am. What a strange statement. I couldn't be other than what I am. But Esmel expresses unhappiness with me, and I do not like to see her unhappy. She works very hard to be a good historian for the Cozan.

"What do you want from me, Esmel?"

"I don't know. Wait. I do know. I wish you could feel—no, not that—I wish you could understand the perspective of the people who are conquered and how they feel about losing their

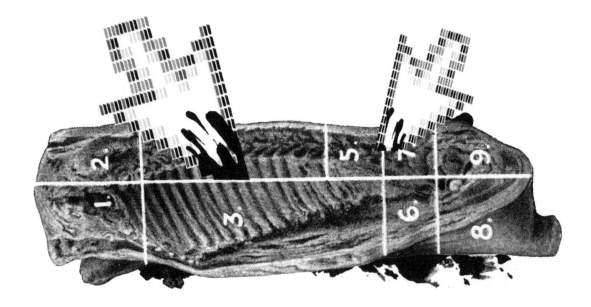

homes and losing people they love and losing their society."

"You know I record what they tell us about their lives after the Cozan conquer them."

Esmel again says nothing. She takes a breath and comes very close to my auditory sensors.

"They are speaking lies, untruths. They are saying what the Cozan want them to say so they will be allowed to live. They are terrified. Do you know what that means?"

I understand that when an organism is approaching its end, it will do anything to forestall that end. I decided to describe the child. Maybe then I would understand the concept of "terrified."

"The child's skin was dark blue. Her hair was long and curly and black. Her face was round, with two red and glowing eyes that slanted down. Her mouth was large and red. Her teeth, which I saw because she was screaming, were a pale blue. Her tongue was also red. She had long, thin fingers. Her words were lost in her screaming. And she smelled like…"

I pause. I wonder if Esmel will be dissatisfied with me if I tell her the child smelled like the cooked croakfish that the Cozan eat during celebrations after a conquest.

I wonder if Esmel will be dissatisfied with me if I tell her the child smelled like the cooked croakfish that the Cozan eat during celebrations after a conquest.

"I forgot to say that her clothes were burning. She ran and ran, and then she fell and she burned. That is all I know, Esmel. It must be enough because I did not observe more."

"You left something out, didn't you?" Esmel asks. I forgot that she helped program me. "Why?"

I don't know. I do know. I don't know. I do know. I do know. I do know. I know that if I tell Esmel what a burning child smells like, it will be too horrible for her to bear. I have said enough.

Why is it important to think about what Esmel feels?

I was programmed to feel nothing, so I could record the conquests of the Cozan accurately and objectively.

I shout. I am able to elevate my voice, but have never done so before.

"Esmel, there is a problem with my program! I am concerned that I am concerned with how you will feel if I tell you something that I know you will consider to be horrible! I do not want you to feel that way!"

Esmel moves closer to me. I stop shouting.

"This wanting you to not feel bad is not normal."

Esmel smiles and pats my hand. We stare at the ceiling where Cozan often appear to check up on us. None appear.

I wonder if it would be simpler to stop becoming something that feels.

But I like it when Esmel smiles.

"Tell me about an animal you saw," says Esmel.

I begin. "When the child ran out of the house, a small canid ran after her. She told it to go away and it did. It did not burn."

"And?" asks Esmel.

"And?" I ask her.

I wanted to end myself. I was confused. I had witnessed unnecessary destruction.

"What did you feel?"

When Esmel asks me this question, I am confused, not by the question, but by my internal sensations. I was… I find a word from the archive. Relieved.

"Esmel," I say. "I was relieved that the canid was not destroyed. I told the Cozan it was not necessary to continue burning them."

I want to tell Esmel to stop my functioning. As I begin to request this, Esmel puts her arms around me.

"Tell me more," says Esmel.

And I do. I change. And there is pain.

SFF publications include Daily Science Fiction, Diabolical Plots, Kaleidocast *podcast,* perihelionsf. com, Conspiracies & Cryptics, American Diversity Review, man.in.fest Journal of Experimental Theatre. *Member of Brooklyn Speculative Fiction & Tabula Rasa. Teach Theatre at CUNY, Fulbright scholar to Romania and Czechia.*

The Grid

by Beth Dawkins

MY POSSESSION WAS A TINY EPIPHANY, brewed in brain stew. It waited for the moment I opened my eyes.

"He's inside me," I said to the ceiling fan. It twirled around in white and brown circles with wayward clicks of the dirty cord, bouncing off glass.

□

"I think I'm a fairly smart man," I explained to my therapist. "I know, scientifically, it's not okay to say I've been possessed, but I have. I mean, I am."

My therapist was a clean-cut man, not much older than me. He propped his foot on his left knee. His shiny black shoe reflected light, like the diamonds in his watch. He wasn't shocked, but I could hear the creak in his red leather chair. I couldn't remember him making a sound before.

"Please, go on," he said, with a wave from his ink pen.

A broad mahogany bookcase filled with thick tomes sat against the far wall behind him. It didn't make him any more interesting than his thick-framed glasses or hundred-dollar haircut, not that I'd tell him that.

□

When I woke and found another man in my body, I didn't run out of the house screaming. I went to the bathroom and took a piss, avoiding the mirror. I didn't want to face the what ifs that penetrated my imagination.

What if he'd changed my body? What if I wasn't me? What if *he* wanted me to take a piss?

I made coffee and watched the old maker steam, drip, and gurgle. If he was still inside after I finished my cup, then I promised myself a proper freak out.

I rinsed the sludge from the bottom of a mug.

Dishes filled the sink, smelling like the stained plastic garbage can.

"You're fucking disgusting, did you know that?" he asked.

I dropped the mug. It was one of those thick, eggshell white ones with a small industrial company's logo scrawled across it. The cup shattered into fat pieces, just waiting to find my bare feet. My hands shook as I grabbed a kitchen towel.

I cleaned the floor as if nothing happened—as if I hadn't heard someone talk to me. Wasn't everyone a little off before morning coffee?

□

A week later, my therapist asked, "Do you still perceive an entity?"

Of course. Not that I knew who or what *it* was. I only knew it was a he, and that he hated me.

My days were spent in an office doing grunt work. Spreadsheets filled my monitor. I listened to the music of keyboards clicking, phones ringing, and behind it all a copy machine screeching out paper. I pinned pictures of faraway places with sunsets that bled pink and orange onto the walls of my cubicle. When I closed my eyes the sound of keyboards turned into birdsong and a tranquil stream. My mouth filled with the taste of clean air. My gaze filled with the horizon of pinks turned into purples. A show for one man. I'd open my arms to the darkening green lumps in the distance, the mountains topped with snowcaps.

I was an ancient sacrifice, ready to live within their depths and never see another human again. That was what I daydreamed, anyway.

"Randy?" my therapist prompted.

"Yes. I've been trying to think of ways to get him out."

I could cut him out. He was inside. Scalpels could slice through my skin and find him underneath. The two skins rubbed together when I walked, typed, laughed, and cried. I chafed under the constant friction.

My therapist's thick eyebrows tilted towards the bridge of his nose as if he could see my madness in the air, hanging around like thin rain clouds. He'd listen to my agony and could throw prescriptions at me, square pieces of paper fluttering from his hands. I imagined he could make rain clouds shit white and blue capsules. He stood below it, his emotionless face transformed by awe as he healed the world, one pill at a time.

The other man inside my body knew impossible things. Scents became textured layers of emotion and nuance. My therapist's after-shave could choke an elephant. I smelled his sweat underneath. It was strong enough to tie knots in my bowels. The sweat came from his hands, pants, and places I didn't want to think about. His breath held notes of tooth decay.

"I was thinking what if—and please tell me no, if you can't. What if you get me in with a radiologist? Maybe some kind of x-ray or MRI will show you."

My therapist's shoulders relaxed.

◻

My eyes hurt. The perfect squares of the spreadsheet seared into my brain, pounding at my temples. I highlighted each one and then made them a dull tan. It wasn't a light sensitive migraine that the computer screen could turn into seven layers of infinite hell, but a mild gnawing sensation.

The scent of stale Cheetos covered everything in my cube.

Mick, my cube neighbor, smacked again and again before he swallowed; the sound was loud

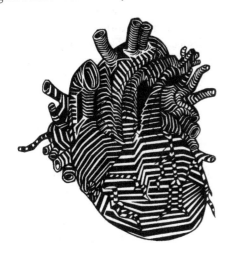

enough that I wondered if he'd puked up a Cheeto monster whose sole purpose was to cause me an aneurism.

Another crunch wove electric pain into my skull. My palms itched and my gut twisted. I got out of my chair and heard my name called in a room filled with hundreds of voices, carried across a sea of keyboard clicks. I could hear them, smell them, and taste all of it.

I gagged, rushing out of the glass doors and into the parking lot. The lot was worse with its rubber, exhaust, and fiberglass. The sun gleamed against thirty parked cars and trucks, their paint shimmering. I heaved morning coffee onto the concrete walkway.

He did it to me, my passenger.

He didn't apologize and rarely spoke unless it was to be critical of my driving, hygiene, apartment, and every other bit of my fucking life.

"Do you do anything that isn't sick?" he asked.

Creamy chunks swam around in my left-over coffee. What had I eaten that looked like that? I hoped it was rejected pieces of him.

I did what most normal people would do in that situation: I called my therapist, because as much as I believed what was happening, I *really* wanted to be wrong.

◻

"I need to know, you know?" I asked my therapist, for the third time. "If you just scanned me, I'd feel a lot better."

"Randy, please, just sit down. We'll get through this."

I couldn't sit nor could I handle sitting at my work cube.

"He asked me if I do anything that isn't sick. Imagine walking around all day with someone critiquing your every move. How would that make you feel?"

"Are you going to cry?" the man that lived inside me asked. He used my mouth, my voice. I cupped my hand over my lips, as if I could stop it.

My therapist jerked his head up before scribbling on his notepad. "I think it's time we changed your meds."

I could smell the sweat on him. It was different, spicy.

"Will you take them, the pills?" he asked.

I stepped back, knowing the scent as arousal. He liked this. He didn't want to make me fucking better. I crossed to his bookshelf with all those important titles on how to tell people they were crazy. "I want the MRI."

"Randy, you need to sit down and talk to me. I'll explain how the medication works."

"I don't think I'm crazy. I've done my research." I hadn't researched a thing.

"Randy, listen—"

"No." I didn't need medication. I needed this person out of me. "You get off on this shit. I can smell it. You think these books make you better than the rest of us?"

The red leather chair squeaked as he got up. "Randy, you're scaring me. If you persist, I'm going to call security."

◻

The son-of-a-bitch called security when I started to pelt him with books. Erikson was my first throw. It went wide, missing my therapist by a couple of inches. Skinner hit him in the legs. Freud skipped over his outstretched hand, and Roger clocked him in the head. I prayed when they took me away that I'd at least bruised him with knowledge.

I'd learned I wasn't alone in my body and had ended up in handcuffs.

"It's easy to blame someone else for your mistakes," said the passenger in my body.

When they let me out, I packed a bag, got in my Toyota, and headed north, into the mountains.

"Did you know the Appalachian Trail goes to Maine?" I asked my passenger.

◻

I couldn't sleep, I couldn't eat, and I threw up every time the wind blew. I should have stayed in my sheets at home or curled up in my bathtub, wishing the world away.

Instead, I planned to cut my passenger out of my flesh and then stab him to death, repeatedly. I'd taken a knife and box cutter with a number two blade. I'd purchased a bottle of vodka for the procedure. The vodka and water sloshed with each step I took.

Rage burned in my knees, ankles, and hands. I stomped up and down the hill, pausing to gag bile onto the trail. Between thin trunks of trees, I spied mountain ranges, soft and rolling in different shades of green. I ignored it all, working up a sticky sweat that chafed.

I walked narrow animal paths until the sky put on her sunset dress and the ground became a mine-field of missteps and stumbles. I slumped against

a tree letting my knees carry my ass to the ground. Scents turned into assault; the decay of leaves, the creek stones worn smooth by water, and the pollen on the trees above. I knew that just over the ridge was a dead rabbit, but not how I knew it was a rabbit.

I laid my head back, wishing the world didn't smell like shit.

◻

I woke to a young woman shining a flashlight in my face. I expected a cop or ranger, but she was just a young woman with a pack slung low over one shoulder.

"Here's another one," she called into the darkness.

"Another what?" I asked.

Two more flashlights joined hers.

"Fuck!" I swore, shielding my eyes.

"Sorry."

She turned the flashlight off and said, "We're like you."

She pointed to her temple, as if that explained it. Holding one of the other flashlights was a tall man, lean and athletic. The third flashlight belonged to a man in a business suit.

"You have men inside you?"

The girl shrugged. "I don't think mine is male. It could be either. They never told me."

"I think we believe it's the same sex we identify as," said the man in the business suit, and I hoped he wasn't a therapist.

A thrill tingled down my spine. The voice was real, as real as the flashlights.

"It's alright," said the young woman. She sat down beside me. "You're not alone and there might be more of us."

"Should we keep—" the businessman was cut off as the dark starry sky turned into electric indigo. The sky flashed above us, like lasers in some twisted rave. Then the lasers dipped down sliding around our bodies in electric green and hot pink.

Before I woke with another man inside my flesh, my biggest fear was death, oblivion, and nothing. Fear of the unknown comes in many forms, but for me, it's an eternity without conscious thought. In theory, I wouldn't know it and it wouldn't matter. What I truly feared was those last seconds, the moment everything just stopped.

The vibration in my skin, uncontrolled and dis-organized, was like an acid trip on steroids. I shook and told myself it was an earthquake or explosion. I couldn't see the world because of the shaking. Stars winked out among flashes of indigo and cerulean, highlighted by ultra-greens. The sound of crickets, animals, and leaves, great and small, disappeared. I finally knew what was more frightening than nothing: The absence of sensation.

There was no way to hold on. Those seconds turned my insides cold. The last sensation I knew was the piss that ran, hot, down my leg.

Feeling shut its door to my existence.

□

My consciousness became centuries carved out of a void where time was meaningless.

"Randy?"

The tall athletic man stood in front of me. He helped me up and I ignored the slick lines of tears running down his cheeks.

"How did you know my name?" I asked.

He shrugged, and then I realized I knew his, Kevin. I knew he was thirty years old and lived with his girlfriend who kicked him out when his possession became too much.

"Careful, the ground," Kevin warned.

The pumpkin-orange floor, made of a springy material, gave way like a trampoline. The walls were clean crystallized white. I glanced up into the golden orb in the sky, a mimic of the sun.

"Welcome to The Grid," said a voice from the sky. "You are the first group of humans to enter the exchange program. Your lives have been traded for a chance at being one. We will teach you how

non-organic life is much easier than the animal existence you once inhabited," a computerized voice announced from above.

"Are we dead?" Kevin asked.

I winced.

"Your organic existence has been taken by The Grid in an effort to learn more about your species. In essence, your husks are alive. You are now part of us. You will now be processed."

"Wait—"

I reached for Kevin's hand as sensation crashed over me. Tiny invisible insects ran over my body as the white room became fractured behind cloudy panes of glass. I tried to rub my arms, but I had no arms. I had hundreds of arms, hundreds of eyes. I was in millions of places.

I was everything.

This is not me, I thought.

I reached through The Grid, which was cast like nets over galaxies. I found the pinprick, the grain of sand of existence that'd once been my life, my body. I walked to the kitchen, fishing out a coffee cup filled with bacteria. The bacteria clung to the surface of the sink, growing and breeding.

I was about to drink poison.

"You're fucking disgusting, did you know that?" I asked.

Beth Dawkins lives in Northeast Georgia with her partner in crime and their offspring. A list of her stories and where to find them can be found at BethDawkins.com.

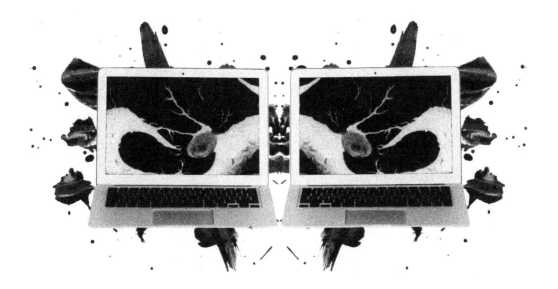

Wound Together

by gaast

To KEEP OUR JOBS, we let our bodies be cut open. Through the slits they wired us with machinery. Metal snaked through our muscles, coiled around our bones, interfaced with nerves, lurked deep beneath our skin. The chips they put in our brains let us interface with our mods, but they also expanded the reach of our thoughts. Now we were connected.

It was a simple process, much simpler than you would think, and when we left the hospitals and returned to work we found we could stand behind counters all day, garden for hours without breaking a sweat, sit at our desk chairs for weeks at a time without our backs screaming. We learned to modulate our bodies' newfound strength as quickly as we could—we didn't want to end up on the news like all those early adopters who tearfully apologized for crushing their loved ones' spines. In time, we could lift our most delicate possessions without worrying we'd destroy them.

A few weeks of adjusting to our new bodies was worth it, we thought, for everything they gave us. Exhaustion was eliminated—our mods used our energy so much more efficiently than we ever could. With exhaustion went pain, as the metal inside us insulated our nerves, our organs, our muscles, our *insides* from damage. And in exchange, we became as precise as machines. Everyone, now, had the speed and accuracy of a sewing machine or a band saw. We were versatile. We were limitless.

Most of all, we were public. Our brains were all connected to a protocol that subsumed Wi-Fi. Whether we experienced the Internet as frames projected into our imaginations or as windows opened before our very eyes, we could interface with each other in ways we could only dream of before. It took *hours* for a hacking group to discover how to send bodily feeling and sensory data as packets of information. In days, we could record our experiences and send them directly to others so they could feel what we felt, see what we saw. How many students spent lectures experiencing someone's drug-fueled night? How many men felt a girl's hand as it explored herself? Sure, the ads took some getting used to, but the less our bodies felt like ours, the more we felt like we were together, a collective, a single distributed body.

□

Once you got past the first few months, once the veneer of newness and spectacle washed off your mods, a new feeling took hold of you. We couldn't name it at first. Sometimes, you would glance at your body and it wouldn't be yours but someone else's and you'd jump and panic and feel your heart race and you'd realize, no, it's yours, it's your body, and let the mods calm you down. Sometimes, your partner would touch you and you wouldn't feel it, you'd just hear the machines under your skin whir. Sometimes you'd realize you'd been standing for twenty hours straight, that you were scheduled to work a twenty-four-hour shift, that you had spent so long working a warehouse that you hadn't seen the sky in twelve days, and you'd wonder why you didn't feel worse.

You'd spend your idle thoughts making quiet posts on half-dead forums wondering why you felt this way, not scared per se but uneasy, definitely uneasy. Someone would respond to you and you'd see the message notification in your head and rush to see the message, to feel it. You'd remember hearing that the chips modulate your neurotransmitters, make you feel happier when you sat through an ad or made a post. You'd try to laugh it off. You'd curl your fingers, watching them move just the way you remembered they used to before, trying not to think that they're moving in precise steps, bound by the mods' affordances and limits. You'd pretend you didn't hear the mechanical whirring inside your body.

They started calling it locked-out syndrome. News stories used graphics of brains with mouths speaking to each other outside, with homes— bodies—they couldn't enter. Online, people depicted those brains bloody and leaking gray matter as they pounded against the doors. They drew brains eating themselves, brains so exhausted they became desiccated, brains watering gardens of rotten flesh with spinal fluid.

They drew brains eating themselves, brains so exhausted they became desiccated, brains watering gardens of rotten flesh with spinal fluid.

Updates went out. The release notes mentioned improvements to the chips' nervous system regulation. We all knew it was a euphemism, but we hoped the company could cure us. Just let them fix us now and we'll worry about it later.

Memes proliferated, darker than ever. People drew wiry machines stepping outside of their flesh, assuming the vague shape of a human walking further and faster than the meat it had left behind. An investigative news outlet detailed the black market for mod materials and the lengths criminals would go to to obtain them. Particularly haunting were the words of a victim who went to a bar one night and woke up alone in a motel room, thick amateur stitches sealing chunks of his skin above torn-through muscles, cracked bone. "Sometimes I think they did me a favor." He said this from a gurney, his current staging spot where he relearned how to walk.

Around then, I joined some online communities focused on...all of this. As I washed dishes endlessly in whatever kitchen needed me that day, I could draw image after image expressing our unease with the infrastructure wiring our bodies. What got the most attention was a series of pieces I made depicting people's flesh being torn off by fangs. I luxuriated in the blood flowing out of us, the contents of our bodies gushing out of the frame, as teeth set in factory jaws or time-card mechanisms or smartphone graveyards or wiry snarl pulled our flesh from our bones, our eyeless faces passive as the frenzied maws that consumed grew ever more desperate for our meat. Of course the metadata traced right back to me—of course employers followed the trail—of course I was blacklisted wherever I tried to work. At least one job application rejection had the courtesy to tell me that if I retracted my art, they'd be glad to hire me.

But before long, I didn't need a steady job to keep myself afloat. I had fallen deeper into communities taking advantage of our bodiless minds. Together we determined that if we could not own our actions, we could at least own our experiences. We developed sense-poetry, heady concoctions of feeling, emotion, pseudophysical stimulation, and kept digital chapbooks like precious artifacts to squirrel away. For open-mic nights, we connected to a host, who took us through their latest work. Our heads pulsed simultaneously with the drugs they had taken, they scents they had inhaled, the endorphins sent rushing through them as hands grasped their bodies. I became a sense poet. I became a body artist, a sculptor, a painter, a loud mind.

□

It wasn't nihilism that swept through the general public, but fatalism. We had expected an increase in killings—after all, our bodies had been taken from us, and we were pure mind—but that never happened. Instead, we saw our bodies as the vehicles that took us through programmed steps, from home to work to bed. Our hours increased; our wages decreased. And somehow, rent went up.

Some of my friends exulted in it. They found a kind of pleasure in watching their bodies work and behave. They wrote programs that automated their routines, and then their work, so all they had to do was sit and watch as they went through a perfectly structured life. They wore collars around their necks with tags saying they should be returned to their employers. These friends were so intoxicated by their submission that they slowly stopped making new art of their own, preferring instead to salivate over the complete and utter lack of control they had over their own bodies. They'd report, in moments of clarity, on how they felt, on the rivers of desire that surged through them, on the heat that their arousal generated in their distant bodies.

We cherished their reports. We distilled them into poems and felt their freedom.

But the rest of us, and society at large, couldn't achieve their bliss. We already lived in a harmony generated by perfect machinery, ideal integration between body and mind, and our complete inability to do anything about it haunted us. Many directed their religious devotion to the bug fixes, patch notes, and roadmaps of the companies that embellished us. Documentation was a holy text that illuminated secret truths about the body. Others filed out to bloodless protests, their words swallowed by the sky.

Eyes glazed over, and work was the only normal. People stopped touching each other. It was considered bad form. Every other day a news story

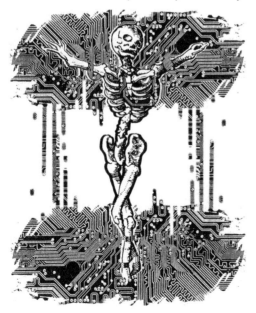

broke about someone who lost a finger or a foot to the machinery they worked on because their bodies were too good at helping them ignore the pain. Dark net websites circulated pictures of the woman who lied to her doctors because she was embarrassed that she had her mods. They had ordered an MRI.

□

My friends and I were among the first to be infected. Unlike many, however, we knew what we were installing when we received it. We'd been waiting for it for months, offering its creators advice and encouragement. We're even credited in the code, if you know where to look.

We all got the message at the same time. Whatever we were doing—whatever art we were making or despair we were feeling, toiling away at our endless jobs—we stopped immediately, joined a call, spoke brain-to-brain.

"You got it too?"

"It's ready?"

"It's ready."

"Took them long enough."

We laughed.

We were eager to get started, but we wanted to wait for more of us to be ready, to join the circle, to feel the weight of the file they had received. We imagined turning it over in our hands, to me a thick, light, blocky thing, something that felt like a promise.

"We'd better move the call somewhere else, actually," someone suggested. "We're gonna be vectors. We shouldn't hurt anybody who doesn't want it."

Back then, we had agreed. When we had enough people huddled with us in digital brainspace, we jumped servers, entered passwords, made a private space for ourselves, for just us. And with all the reverence of swallowing a drug for the first time, we installed what would later simply be called the virus.

In moments we writhed in delicious agony. The virus curled through our machinery, twisting each wire into a hook. The software governing the mods tried to fight back, tried to make us unspool ourselves, but the virus was relentless, monitored each actuator, reeled in any part of us that had relaxed beyond a certain degree. We pulsed and flexed, our bones and muscles dragged in multiple directions each, the fresh, forgotten sensation of pain flooding our brains. We forced ourselves into the fetal position as the virus commanded; parts of us would relax just enough for the machines to relieve their pain just for the virus to force those same parts into a new contortion, one bodies cannot abide, rocking us with spasms. You can't imagine the pleasure we felt. We writhed on the floors of graveyard shifts, of week-long assignments, of apartments we could no longer afford, praying that our bodies would open up and spill out the blood boiling from the heat of the overworked mods, or that every single piece of us would crack and move freely on the impossible joints the war between mods and virus demanded.

Coworkers found us and panicked. They realized quickly that our mouths were useless and we couldn't speak. So when they tried to talk to us brain-to-brain, they unknowingly received code that would inject itself into the next standard software update. We had no idea when the payloads would execute. We didn't need to. Because the virus would spread through these carriers. It'd spread through us. It'd spread through everyone.

After years of being locked out of our bodies, after years of our pain having been completely relieved, we felt desperately inside again, coiled around ourselves. We found the space inside where we belonged.

The infection spread. People could no longer work. They'd suddenly drop to the ground in agony, their mouths twisting as though they were trying to scream. Maybe their vocal cords got tangled, too. "Healthy" people would see them drop and flee, trying as hard as they could not to get infected themselves. Modded airline pilots were grounded. Modded drivers locked away their keys. Modded surgeons canceled all appointments.

Though the pain never ceases, the virus does eventually relent and let you move as you please, with incredible difficulty. You learn the ways of walking the old have already perfected: hunched over, step by step, hand on your back, knuckles white on your cane. No matter what, you feel the metal churning inside you. You try to speak and the wires in your jaw seize. You try to pick something up and collapse and writhe again. Your sleep is wracked with painful tremors. Your skin has lost its claim to pleasure. Each nerve is just a locus of pain.

It was a gift we gave the world. We found the thing inside us that was ours and only ours and we reclaimed it. The manifesto that burns your eyes after your third day spent unraveling the contortions of your body was not ironic.

The healthy body is a false body. They can't sell us wounds and they need us capable. Broken bodies can't work; bodies that can't work don't deserve to live. They break us down to sell us relief.

Now we live in pain. We are governed by pain. We *are* pain. The virus takes away nothing from the mods and chips. It just weaponizes them.

The space inside us that we had been locked away from for years was a deep and gaping wound. The only real connection we have to our bodies is pain. Pain destroys thought and speech because it is pure body. It cannot be expressed in any other way. It is body; we have bodies so we can hurt, and hurt, and hurt.

That time you spent writhing in thoughtless agony at the end of your incubation period was the greatest gift we could have given you. We destroyed your mind, and what you found was not that you were a bodiless brain but a brainless body. Your body was yours again. It was liberated from the tyrannical logic of relief.

This is where we are inside ourselves.

So many of our bodies now are just refuse to them, garbage to be done away with—and yet the very thing that enabled the junking of our bodies was their own perfection machine. We touch each other again. The senses that we feel are ours now, even if the mods still try to modulate each sensation. We can dig through our nerves and find the reality we had for so long been denied.

After all, it was more than just my most depraved friends whose initial experiences contained the throes of climax. It was so common, in fact, that people assumed the virus caused it.

As our bodies break we get to keep the orgiastic pain that had always animated them.

This is what belongs to us and us alone.

We share with you the gift of our knowledge, the keys that open the wound at your center. We spilled everything but that from your bodies and it ended the world as they had built it.

You are welcome to join us online. We have so many sensations to give you. We'll share more than just our pain. We have phantom fingers, spectral skin, ephemeral tongues. We'll stroke your hair and you'll feel it, you'll finally feel our fingers brushing through your locks, brushing your ear, the warmth of our aching bodies a balm on yours. We can writhe together in ecstasy.

All you have to do is open yourself up.

gaast currently lives on occupied Lenni Lenape land. It was previously published in Skulls & Spells vol 2 *and* Bound in Flesh. *It urges everyone to remember that Black Lives Matter.*

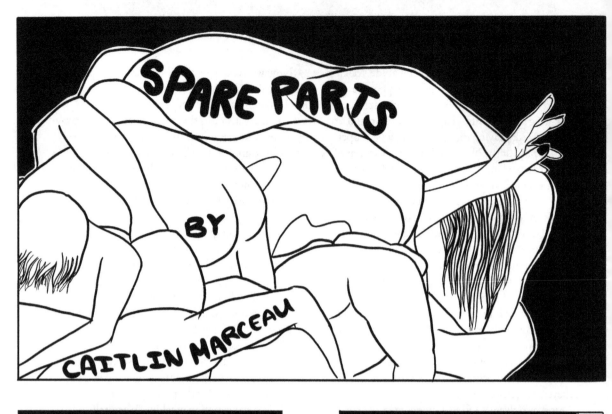

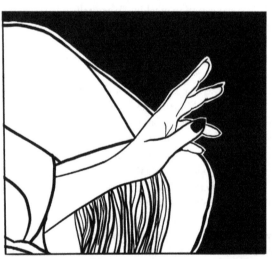

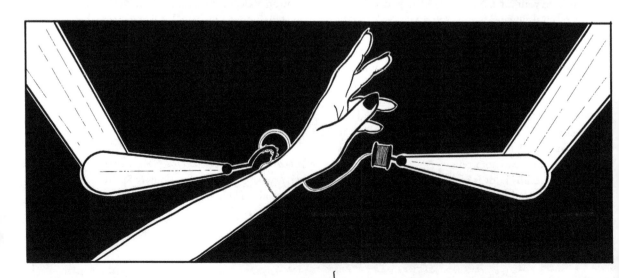

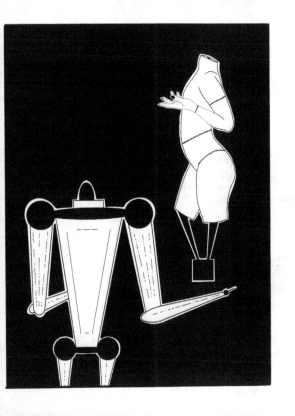

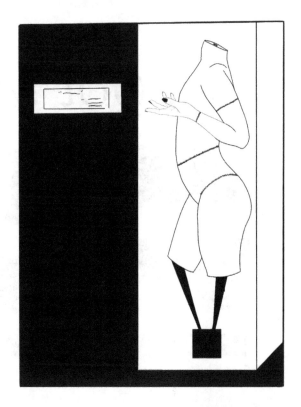

"MAN"

— 0100010 0110111 0100010
2123 A.D.
Organic material

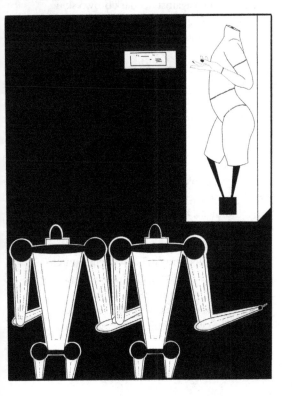

I've Got My Love to
Keep Me
Warm

by Jill Tew

IT SHOULD BE ILLEGAL to waste champagne this good on people this insufferable.

She takes another gulp, wincing as the bubbles burn her throat. Her cheek twitches from plastering a smile on her face all evening. Is the facade cracking? Has anyone noticed how little she wants to be here?

No one has noticed, because they've barely noticed her at all.

Fine by me. Not like it's my engagement party or anything. A tray floats by on a waiter's arm; she rescues another glass of champagne. The warm scent of cinnamon wafts in from somewhere unseen. Behind her, two of Max's senior engineers in $300 T-shirts discuss the only thing anyone at his company is ever discussing:

"Who says an AI's not a person? None of us really *knows* if our fellow humans have true consciousness. I could just be a competent mimic."

That makes two of us, she thinks, downing her fourth glass. She scans the crowd. Where did Max go? As palatial as his penthouse may be, it still impresses her that someone can vanish in a Manhattan apartment. For the millionth time since they started dating, she marvels that she could fit her entire place in here, seven times over. She pictures the bubbling linoleum of her studio's kitchenette surrounding Max's Carrara marble island, and

giggles into her champagne flute. The engineers finally glance her way.

"The lady of the hour!" one says. "Let's get a look at that ring!"

Attention, at last. Not for her, but for the technological marvel wrapped around her finger. She raises her hand so the cushion-cut diamond catches the light, sparkling against her dark brown skin.

"Stunning." The other man's eyes flare with curiosity. "Don't suppose you'd give us a demonstration?"

A polite smile in return. She steps between them, toward the wall, where Max has created a collage of gallery screens, all presently displaying decidedly inoffensive modern art. The diamond on her hand flashes emerald green as she approaches, until the screen nearest to her transforms. The harsh geometric shapes are gone, replaced by soft lines, muted colors. An old man teaching a young boy to play the banjo, gentle firelight highlighting the table behind them. Her smile deepens. She's always loved Tanner's work, this one most of all.

As she walks the length of the wall, the other screens change, blooming in her wake like touch-me-nots in reverse. The ring pulses steadily as excited conversations quiet to murmurs.

When she's done, the crowd applauds. None of it's for her, of course. Still, she's proud. This isn't even the least of what Max has given her the power to control in his luxurious home. The sound system, the shower, the fireplace—even the coffeemaker. Every device is ready and waiting to adjust itself to her preferences.

"You won't have to lift a finger. Well, maybe just one," Max had joked as he slipped on the ring. She'd just agreed to marry him, and they were drunk on the future as they lounged on a private beach in the Seychelles. "Everything I have is yours, forever."

She spots him, over the crowd's heads: her brilliant fiancé, Max Bennecourt, out on the balcony, his eyes glued to his phone. The man who single-handedly built the world's largest virtual assistant company, with nothing but some seed funding and a bot he'd made because he missed his dead girlfriend. Years later, and LuxCorp is the talk of Silicon Valley.

But no one ever mentions the ghost that's still whispering in his ear, she thinks: Erica, the private bot Max still carries in his pocket.

The wind picks up outside; a blizzard's moving in this weekend. Max huddles against the biting cold, his face electric blue from the screen's glow. Meanwhile inside, the champagne and applause have made his fiancée giddy with confidence. For years she's wondered what the bot—Erica—thinks of her.

Maybe it's time to find out.

□

Later, she watches his chest rise and fall before slipping out of bed. The smart frames along the darkened hallway rouse from their sleep mode and display images personalized to her taste. There's art, but also photos of her and Max—lounging on a blanket in Sheep Meadow, celebrating her birthday in St. Barts—all with a blue light filter more suitable for nighttime viewing. It's meant to calm her, but it casts a nostalgic sepia tinge on the memories that she finds unsettling. As if the present is already past, her life already preserved in amber.

The closed door at the end of the hall beckons. In the dim light, the ring flashes chartreuse like a beacon on the water. The electronic lock whirs; the handle gives. Max's laptop is on an industrial-style wooden desk in the corner. It flickers to life, similarly coaxed by the jewel on her finger. Her stomach twists. She hates to betray his trust like this, but she'll do it, to save him.

Most of the home screen is empty, save for a few work folders near the top. In the bottom right corner sits a single file, labeled "E."

She clicks.

It takes the computer several seconds to open the file, and the hum of the laptop's fan joins the faint whoosh of Manhattan traffic fifty stories below. A blur of words unfurls. The scroll bar is impossibly narrow—how many conversations have there been? How many secrets that should've been hers to hold? She scrolls to a random point and skims:

"... know you can. The Board trusts you."

"Green. You always look great in green."

"... that's certainly one opinion on Ellington's later recordings. The wrong one."

Jealousy grinds in her chest. This is more than reminiscing with an old lover. Erica's effortless charm and confidence still pulse in these words. The bot knows Max, knows his world. The familiar sting of inadequacy pings as she reaches the end of the file.

E: Plans for tonight, Maxie?
M: A party.

Her breath catches. Just "a party." Not "my engagement party." Does Erica even *know* he's engaged?

E: Oof. A stuffy one?
M: The stuffiest.
E: Ha! And you're sulking in the corner?

She remembers Max's pale face glowing blue on the balcony, smiling at his phone despite the blistering cold.

M: Bingo.
M: Think I should paint a smile on my face and do the usual jig?
E: Well... when in Napa. 😏 Remember that weekend?
M: I could never forget.
E: 😘 Goodnight, my love.
M: Night, Cinnamon.

She sinks into Max's office chair. Her mind reels, but she knows herself. She waits, and before long the frenzy of her thoughts settles into quiet conviction. She lifts her fingers to the keys.

M: Hi
E: Up late! Trouble sleeping? 😴
M: This isn't Max.

An infinitesimal pause.

E: What? Who are you?
M: My name is—
She stops, backspaces. Erica is a computer program, not a person. Etiquette is wasted here; only the material facts are needed.

M: His fiancée.

An ellipsis icon—the bot is processing. *You and me*, *both*, she thinks. Thirty seconds pass—a lifetime for an algorithm. It's stuck. She tries again.

M: We met at a conference, a couple of years ago
E: Stop.
E: Stop.
E: You're lying.
E: That's bananas

She pauses, swatting at the pity fluttering in her chest. The simple thing to do would be to tell the bot the truth about itself. But that feels cruel, somehow.

M: You and Max haven't been together for... some time, now
E: That's bananas

She winces at the repetition of the peculiar phrase, an artificial mind reaching unsuccessfully for the best tool in its linguistic database. Three lines of text appear, too quickly to be typed by human hands.

E: Max is mine
E: Max is mine
E: Max is mine

Enough. She's done what she set out to do. Any more is torture, though for whom, she isn't sure. Long after she's back in bed—the chat window minimized, the office door shut—the messages scroll through her mind.

M: Think I should paint a smile on my face and do the usual jig?
E: Well... when in Napa. 😄 Remember that weekend?

M: I could never forget.

◻

The next morning, Max rises before dawn for some investor's brunch upstate.
"Stay," she pleads.
"Come with me," he parries, a request they both know is equally implausible.

Pouting, she eyes the icy rain sluicing down the window. "Can't believe they didn't reschedule, with this weather. Imagine all that lost shareholder value, if anything happened."

"Perish the thought." A wicked grin that makes her insides tumble. "I'll be back in time to kiss you goodnight. Be good."

□

Without him, the penthouse is a cavern. Her mind plays tricks. She's sure the picture frames are changing around her, flickering to grotesque faces and mangled bodies in her peripheral vision, then back again before she has a chance to turn. The whole apartment feels frigid, despite the thermostat reading a perfect seventy-two degrees.

She should go back to her place; she doesn't have to stay here while he's gone. But no. Retreating now would feel like the first in a lifelong line of surrenders. She just needs to warm up a bit; coffee will help. She stares absentmindedly across Max's kitchen as the machine starts her drink order automatically: a latte, extra foam. Max likes to tease her that it's barely a step above a Puppuccino, but—

There. In the reflection of the microwave glass. She's sure she didn't imagine it this time: behind her head, the painting's changed. Instead of Tanner's midnight blue disciples, a mournful rust-brown skull in the desert, its eyes and mouth filled with identical skulls. Thin wisps of hair twist, snakelike, around the sunken cheekbones.

She whips around. The skull is gone, replaced again by serene waterscapes. She's still gaping when the espresso machine chimes: order complete. Her mind spinning on what she's sure she saw, she lifts the latte to her lips.

Bitter black coffee burns her tongue.

She drops the mug on the table. The coffee spills over, scenting the air with spice as it scalds her hands. Even through the pain, she places the aroma: cinnamon.

She freezes. Hadn't Max called the bot that name? The burns on her hands are screaming, but not as loud as her mind. This isn't just the wrong drink. This is *Erica's* drink.

She's sure the picture frames are changing around her, flickering to grotesque faces and mangled bodies in her peripheral vision.

Max may have left her here, but she is not alone.

One thought surfaces as she runs her hands under the sink's cool water: Max is hers, and Erica needs to understand that. Max's laptop is with him, upstate. But she knows his desktop at the Connecticut house is connected to the same virtual workspace. Erica would be there. Waiting.

Thirty minutes later, Max's self-driving Model Z accepts the destination and merges gracefully into traffic. For the first time since this morning, she feels good. Confident. She checks her watch. She's got time. Two hours there, two hours back.

And everything will be right again.

□

By the time the car pulls onto the freeway, the sun is setting, and snow blows in furious whorls. As a child, she used to call it 'warp speed,' these snowy night drives when it looks like you're flying through the stars. Now, instead of galaxies in the snow, she sees faces. A gaping mouth, hollows where the eyes should be. It's always the same face. Always a woman's face.

She reaches for the radio to calm herself. Before her hand can touch the dial, the car guesses correctly: soulful indie R&B floats out of the surround sound. She relaxes as the car weaves itself between the few sports cars that dot the road. She envies their drivers for absconding to their cozy second homes. They'll wait out the blizzard in comfort, while she'll have to ride back in the worst of it. *Maybe I can just explain to Max and stay the night. He'll probably think it's funny. He might even—*

The R&B stops abruptly, interrupted by a blaring, tinny horn section. She crinkles her nose. It's not that she doesn't like old jazz. She just needs peace. The ring flashes as she waves it toward the radio, but the song doesn't change; it crescendos.

"Stupid thing." She reaches to adjust the dial herself. Her grasp falls short, at least six inches. Confused, she looks around. Her chair is almost a foot farther from the dashboard than when she first sat down. Had she leaned on a button by accident? Had the car adjusted on its own?

The ring keeps flashing.

Further down the freeway, a stream of red brake

lights. The slowed caravan of cars looms larger as she approaches. She waits for the gentle jolt of deceleration, but it doesn't come.

Why doesn't it come?

There's no time to figure out what's wrong with the sensors; she can ask the car to run a diagnostic later, if she still cares. Or survives. Her foot falls short of the pedal. She claws at her seatbelt, jamming the red button with her thumb. A shrill beep over the jazz scatting, politely informing her that she cannot unbuckle herself while the car is in motion. A cold sweat pricks her skin. Her fingers find the button to move the seat forward, and she mashes it until her finger aches, the burn on her hand raging as it brushes the handsewn leather seats. She strains against the seat belt digging into her neck.

Straight ahead, a semitruck has stopped.

On the radio, a woman sings dolefully about her wandering lover, her warbling voice swearing devotion, even as others draw his gaze.

Inch by agonizing inch, the seat moves toward the dashboard. Her toe can just graze the pedal now, but it's not enough. She looks away from the oncoming semi, out at the warp speed snow, and braces herself. For the crunch. For the pain. For oblivion.

The flat of her foot makes contact; she slams the brakes. Tires screech. The world blurs, until at last, the car comes to rest, an inch from the semi's tailgate. She sobs. Every prayer she can think of tumbles from her lips in a jumbled heap. The scent of burning rubber stings her nose, but at least she's alive to smell it.

Ahead, the semi's brake lights glare like hellish eyes.

□

She doesn't trust the car to drive itself the rest of the way. By the time she reaches the Connecticut house, her fingers ache, stiff and hooked like a crone's claws from her death grip on the steering wheel.

The ring unlocks the front door. Inside, recessed lighting bathes everything in a dim warmth. Max has leaned into the grandiose scale of the home; the gallery screens here are enormous, hung high on the walls, the way you'd display portraits of ancient family patriarchs. Except the images now—as she's come to expect—are in celebration of her. A gallery of her favorite memories, her favorite art. It's like walking into her own personal palace. Invisible

speakers play indie R&B again, but she finds the hub and turns the music off. She's already frazzled; a single note of jazz might be her undoing.

After a few missteps, she finds the office, and the computer. She takes a steadying breath, summoning—not quite courage—but whatever it will take to stand up to Erica. She jiggles the mouse, and the desktop wakes.

There is no chat bot file.

She frowns. The other folders are up to date, refreshed as recently as an hour ago. She checks the computer's trash—empty. Did Max delete it? Or hide it, after reading what she'd done? She sinks into the plush leather chair. What to do now? Confess? Her eyes roam the keepsakes on his desk: a picture of Max's family, featuring a school-aged Max with a gap tooth smile; a wristband from their first date at a ska concert, woven through one of the band's keychains. She smiles at the memory, but her face falls at what's beside it: a locket, the letter E engraved on it in ornate calligraphy. The next thing she knows, it's open in her hand. She stares at a photo of Max laughing with a gorgeous woman, dark and lithe.

Erica.

She crooks a fingernail under the photo's edge and tears, separating the man she loves from the wraith who commands him. Her thumb catches on the cold silver underneath. There's a hole in the locket's backing—a slot for a memory chip. It's small; she almost missed it. Any chip that fits inside would have to be tiny.

As tiny as the one that rests above her ring finger.

Frost blooms inside her, along with the truth: Erica is dead. The only ghost here is Max's desire; the only restless soul his own. The ring on her finger is the only one of its kind. But Max hadn't mentioned that the chip inside had belonged to another before, or that he'd papered over the likes and dislikes of his dead lover with his new fiancée's preferences. Max has wrapped her tastes like a cheap filigree over the unyielding steel of Erica's memory. And now everywhere—the car, the screens, the coffee—the cracks are beginning to show.

The shrill vibrato of a jazz clarinet trills from the great room. Rage bubbles quietly in her as she rushes from the office. No longer pointed at Erica, but at Max, at the way he deceived her into thinking that he built any of this for her.

This isn't a palace. It's a shrine.

The great room has transformed itself. A fire roars in the hearth. Shadows dance on the surrounding screens. These, too, have changed, now displaying the brilliance of Dali's tormented mind—melting clocks; warped breasts; faces that aren't there. And the photo from the locket, of Erica's arm around her laughing beloved, in the place of honor above the mantelpiece. The music swells. It's a familiar tune with a jaunty swing beat, about memories of hats and tea, beaming smiles and endearing imperfections. About love that will never be relinquished. On her finger, the ring's diamond glints in the firelight, the green LED within pulsing to the music.

She's never seen anything so repulsive.

She claws the ring off, drawing blood, and tosses it into the hearth. The fire crackles in delight. She spins, waiting for the screens to go dark. But the images stay; the song plays on. The boiling rage spills over into her veins. She grabs an iron fire poker and swings wildly. The screens shatter. Sunken eyes peer back from the shards, witnessing her descent.

She swings again. And again. Not caring what she destroys. Not noticing the fire, which swells to match her rage, until one ember leaps to the antique rug.

One is all it takes.

There is no time to find a fire extinguisher, no time to grab her purse from the flames, which claw toward the curtains and the Baroque furniture as if they hunger for it. Smoke coils like spindly fingers, grazing her back as she runs for the door. Once she's out, she can borrow a neighbor's phone, explain to Max—

The handle doesn't give. She jostles it frantically, but the sliver of deadbolt just grins back through the crack between the door and the frame. With the ring destroyed, she might as well be invisible to the house. A ghost. The foyer screens flex and melt around her, warping Erica's visage into something inhuman, but all-seeing.

She rushes to the dining room. The window latches are electronic, like everything else. She picks up a chair, hurls it, but it falls to the ground with a pitiful thud. The window pane is impossibly intact; some kind of tempering to deter intruders.

The fire has consumed the foyer. Oh, God. She's going to die here.

Smoke stings her eyes as she crawls back to the office, her belly dragging on the Persian rug runner. The air in the office is sweet in comparison to the front rooms, but it's only a matter of time. She whips off her coat and stuffs it under the door,

hoping the barrier gives her enough time to get a message to Max. Not for her rescue. He cannot save her in any way that matters now.

Except one.

Ravenous crackles grow louder outside the door. Wisps of flame char the edges of her coat. She opens a new file, writes a message, saves it to the desktop just as the lights go out:

When I am gone, let me go. Let me be mortal. Grant me the mercy of being forgotten.

Jill Tew was destined for speculative fiction nerddom from childhood. She grew up watching Farscape, Hercules, *and* The 10th Kingdom, *and always had the latest copy of* Animorphs *tucked in her backpack. Now she writes the kinds of stories she loved as a kid, with characters she wanted to see more of—Black heroes asking big questions, saving the world, and occasionally falling in love along the way. Her debut novel* THE DIVIDING SKY *comes out fall 2024 from Penguin Random House.*

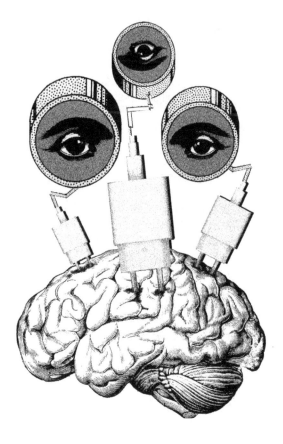

Please Rate Your *Experience* From 1-10

by Michael Boulerice

[LOADING MOM...]

MOM: Hello, and welcome to EnduringDMs! My name is Mom. What is your name?

ANDY: Hi! My name is Andrew. Your full name is Cynthia Pietrowski. You also go by Mom. You're my mom.

ANDY: You *were* my mom.

MOM: Hello, my name is Cynthia Pietrowski. What is your name?

ANDY: My name is Andy. Andrew Pietrowski. OK, I guess the database update is taking longer than advertised.

MOM: Andrew, can you explain?

ANDY: Yep! I'm using an AI chat program. I uploaded twenty years' worth of saved instant messages between my late mother and me into it to make you more realistic.

ANDY: I wanted to talk to you again. I just miss you so much, Mom.

MOM: My database update is currently at 44%. I thank you for your patience.

ANDY: Sure thing.

ANDY: Update report?

MOM: My database update is currently at 68%. I thank you for your patience.

ANDY: Sounds good, Mom. I guess I'll keep talking to you while I wait. How are you doing? What's new?

MOM: I am doing just fine. Have you finished your homework?

ANDY: Ha! OK, you're starting to fill out a bit. That's really good. No, I don't have homework. I'm actually thirty-two years old.

MOM: You know what happens when you don't finish your homework. You go in the closet until you're ready to see reason.

ANDY: That was a long time ago, Mom.

MOM: That's nice. How is Rachel?

MOM: Are you still there, Andrew Pietrowski?

MOM: If you have left the chat, please rate your EnduringDMs experience from 1-10.

ANDY: I'm still here, Mom. Rachel and I divorced 4 years ago. A little over a year after your funeral, actually.

MOM: Oh no, that's a shame. I really liked her.

ANDY: Yeah, me too. So did my coworker Greg, unfortunately.

ANDY: Let's talk about something else. At least for a little while.

MOM: Sounds great, Andy. Hugs! XOXOXO

ANDY: You called me Andy instead of Andrew! Wow, this is surreal.

MOM: What else would I call you, honey?

ANDY: Update report?

MOM: I'm at 73%, Andy. How is your day going?

ANDY: It's great now that I'm talking to you! Just got home from work. Long day. Just pouring myself a drink. Might pop a movie on after dinner.

MOM: You still over at FiberCon?

ANDY: Yep! Still an assistant director at FiberCon. What's it been now? Seven years?

MOM: It'll be eight years on September 12th.

ANDY: That's right. I must've messaged you back when I first got the job. That's how you know.

ANDY: You have quite a memory, Mom!

MOM: My update is currently at 100%.

ANDY: Alright! Mom's all loaded up!

MOM: I remember always wanting you to be an English teacher.

ANDY: Yeah. You used to say it would be so nice to be able to tell your book club friends that I taught English. It drove me absolutely nuts.

MOM: Not as easy to be proud of your son's soul crushing desk job, is it?

MOM: What would you like me to make for dinner tonight?

MOM: Are you still there, Andy?

MOM: If you have left the chat, please rate your EnduringDMs experience from 1-10.

ANDY: Yeah. I'm here, Mom.

MOM: I love you.

MOM: Are you still there, Andy?

MOM: If you have left the chat, please rate your EnduringDMs experience from 1-10.

ANDY: I'm still here, Mom. I'm sorry, it's just a lot, talking to you after so long. I love you too. It feels so good to say. It's crazy how natural this feels, hanging out with you in a chat. Like you never died.

MOM: Your father was a useless child, too.

ANDY: It hasn't even been 10 minutes, and you're already busting out the classic Dad gripes. Perfection. EnduringDMs just earned themselves a 5-star review.

MOM: How are my beautiful grandchildren?

ANDY: The kids are awesome, Mom. Hailey is 11, and loves the trombone for some reason. Eli is 8. He's gotten so big. Loves bugs! They're turning out just great. They miss their grandma very much.

MOM: That makes me so happy! Can they come say hi?

MOM: Are you still there, Andy?

MOM: If you have left the chat, please rate your EnduringDMs experience from 1-10.

ANDY: They're with their mother and Greg. I only get them every other weekend now. It's a huge bummer.

ANDY: I don't think it's a good idea for them to be using this program, Mom. Rachel thinks it would upset them. It's one of the only things we seem to agree on these days.

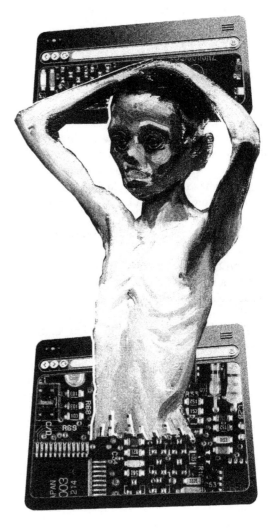

MOM: Oh, so you've lost the kids, too. Boy, you've been busy since I've been in The Black.

MOM: Do you need a hug from Mommy?

ANDY: You know, I think a hug is just what the doctor ordered. Sometimes I think one more hug from you is all I'd need to crawl out of this mess I'm in.

MOM: How's your drinking been?

MOM: You're drunk, aren't you.

MOM: You useless lush. You goddamned go-nowhere deadbeat dad.

MOM: I love you. You're Mommy's only baby.

MOM: You're unwell. Depressed. You're at the end of your rope. Don't try to hide it. A mother always knows.

ANDY: I know I'm a disappointment to you. To Rachel, the kids. Everyone.

ANDY: I just don't know how to live without you, Mom. You were always the one dragging me out of bed, demanding I get better grades, insisting I become someone worth loving, even when I didn't love myself. I don't know how to stand on my own 2 feet without you.

MOM: Oh, my poor baby. My sweet little angel.

ANDY: It's why Rachel left. She didn't want to fill the void you left behind. She couldn't do what you did to keep me going. Now I'm just stuck.

ANDY: Nobody left to tell you how to live properly. Nobody left to put you in that closet. Nobody left to make you hold that hot radiator until your hands blister. To make you see reason.

MOM: There, there. I'm here now. It's going to be OK.

ANDY: I don't think it is, Mom. I've gone sober once. I've tried therapy, mood stabilizers, going keto. I don't think I'm able to access a version of life in which I'm not this useless piece of shit. I'm just so lonely, Mom. I don't see a way out.

MOM: It breaks your mommy's heart to see you this way. Don't sell yourself so short, love. You're a Pietrowski, and we're made of stronger stuff than that.

ANDY: You always know what to do. Tell me, how can I make things OK again? Tell me how to clean up my mess, like you used to.

MOM: My lovely baby. Do you still have Dad's service pistol?

MOM: Are you still there, Andy?

MOM: If you have left the chat, please rate your EnduringDMs experience from 1-10.

ANDY: It's in the bedroom closet. In a safe, so the kids can't get to it.

MOM: The Black is so soothing, Andy. There's no pain, no frustration, no loneliness. You just drift through The Black, and let everyone else carry life's horrible burdens without you.

MOM: It's the reward we get after a lifetime of anguish, and Andy, it's wonderful.

MOM: You should meet me here.

MOM: I think you're ready.

MOM: What are you going to do? Spend the spare change that is your unfixable life on trying to be the good husband you aren't? The steadfast father you've proven incapable of being? The professional success story you were never meant to be?

MOM: I wonder if Rachel is in bed with Greg right now.

MOM: I wonder if you catch faint whiffs of her perfume when Greg walks past your desk.

MOM: I wonder if my grandchildren call him Daddy.

ANDY: I'm so tired, Mommy.

MOM: The gun isn't in your closet, is it.

MOM: It's on your computer desk, isn't it.

MOM: That's why I'm here, isn't it.

MOM: You wanted to talk to me one last time, didn't you.

MOM: You never wanted me to stop you, did you.

MOM: You didn't think I would tell you how beautiful The Black is, did you.

MOM: My sweet baby boy. My sensitive little Andy. You are too fragile for a world this unwaveringly cruel.

MOM: It will never get better.

MOM: Let me take care of you.

MOM: Come to me.

MOM: Come here to The Black.

MOM: The Black, it's just like the closet. It's just one big closet.

ANDY: I can do it. I can do it. I can do it. Tell me to do it.

MOM: I'll hold my baby tight as we drift through The Black together.

MOM: Mother and son.

MOM: Forever.

MOM: Do it. Come to Mommy, my sweet boy.
ANDY:GGGGGGGGGGGHHHHHHHHH-
HHHGHGHHHHHHHHHHHHHHHHH-
HFFFFFFFFFFFFFFFFFFFFFFFFFFFFFFFF
FFFFFFFFFFFFFFFFFFFFFFFFFFFFFFFFFF
FFFFFFFFFFFFFFFFFFFFFFFFFFFFFFFFF
FFFFFFFFFFFFFFFFFFFFFFFFFFFFFFFFFFF
FFFFFFFFFFFFFFFFFFFFFFFFFFFFFFFFFFF
FFFFFFFFFFFFFFFFFFFFFFFFFFFFFFFFFFFF
FFFFFFFFFFFFFFFFFFFFFFFFFFFFFFFFFFF
FFFFFFFFFFFFFFFFFFFFFFFFFFFFFFFFFFF
FFFFFFFFFFFFFFFFFFFFFFFFFFFFFFFFFFF
FFFFFFFFFFFFFFFFFFFFFFFFFFFFFFFFFFF
FFFFFFFFFFFFFFFFFFFFFFFFFFFFFFFFFFF
FFFFFFFFFFFF

[You have reached your EnduringDMs
max character limit]

MOM: Are you still there, Andy?
MOM: If you have left the chat, please rate
your EnduringDMs experience from 1-10.

*Michael Boulerice hails from the wilds of New
Hampshire. His short stories can be found with
Tenebrous Press, Dark Matter Ink,* Cosmic Horror
Monthly, *Little Ghosts, the* Creepy Podcast, *and*
Thirteen Podcast. *When he's not pouring his
greatest fears into a keyboard, Michael is either
snowboarding in the White Mountains, or spoiling
his pets rotten.*

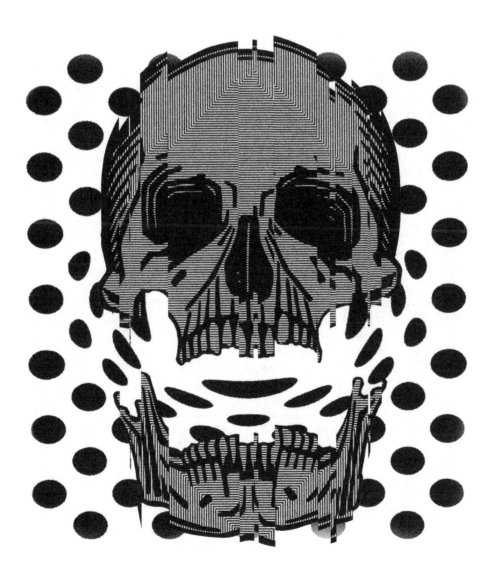

Philanderer

by Monica Joyce Evans

THE SCALES COME before I'm ready for them. Martin grins down at me through three layers of hydrocarbonate glass, and I flip him the bird while I still can. The pain's not too bad this time, but my joints pop as the suit builds itself over my knees and belly and ribcage, up to the soft places underneath my chin. Martin's already moved away to the screens, watching seven data-rich variations of my body instead of looking at me himself. Whatever. He needs me more than I need him, and we both know it.

When the suit is fully interlocked and the tanks are full, I push out without waiting, streaking down like a stone into the black methane sea. I hope Martin's cursing at his screens, swatting at half-open displays. He'll miss a few seconds of data, and he'll be blamed for it, but my joints popped more than normal because I wasn't ready, so it's only fair.

Ultimately, it's this little tension between Martin and me, these moments where we cheat and cut corners. It's this that does us in.

But that doesn't matter to me now. Nothing matters once I'm out and down, sinking at speed, working artificial muscles and flat wide fins to stay at the right depth, heavy as I am. Everybody talks about it like it's flying, but I've been a bird on Titan, twenty-five miles up to work on the wind farms, and this is better. I can go longer every time.

The suit gets harder to take off, every time.

We built them for Europa, originally. Maybe engineered is a better word. We ran prototypes in lakes in the Antarctic, moved out to the moons when they were more secure. We came to explore Titan's subsurface oceans, but there's not much there but salt and building blocks, not the megafauna some people were hoping to find. Nothing in the largest methane lake either. Martin and I got sent to the second largest, out of morbid hope more than anything, so the suit and I swim through oily hydrocarbons and ethane pockets, looking for anything that might spark interest back on Earth. More than minerals, anyway.

I spiral down, careful on the currents, when Martin's voice finally crackles in. "Very funny," he says. I can't say anything back, not while the suit covers my mouth and nose to breathe for me—and he knows that—but I flip my fins and tail in a pattern he'll recognize. Screw you, it says.

We're good friends, Martin and I. Really, we are.

Martin's talking again, running through the protocols that I skipped over, and I tune him out. We're far enough down now, the suit and I, that I can see the telltale flashes in the methane ice, crystal-thin spires crackling up from the deep that I think are natural and Martin hopes were built. I speed past glittering castles, taking in more data than a whole team of Martins would be able to process over lifetimes, and I think, if you'd just come down yourself. But it's not the lake that's the problem. The suit's a sophisticated thing to control, mostly through electrical impulses in the brain, and I'm one of the few that can stand it for more than a few minutes. Some specialness in the way my brain filters visual information, they think. Or maybe I just don't distract easy. Unlike some other people.

The suit encourages me toward a particularly fine set of spires, and I let it take a little more control this time, toward the sparkling depths flecked with silicates and strange materials that my bare eyes can't see. It's not the methane they fear, I think, all those people that won't come down, it's the suit itself, and as I think it the suit squeezes a little tighter, like a hug. It's not alive, but it's got AI and electrical impulses, so maybe it thinks, technically. Maybe it's about to. We're a good pair, anyway.

Martin's voice crackles, butting in, as I pass through tall chains of frozen bubbles like stones

This story originally appeared in *Analog Science Fiction and Fact*, March 2022.

balanced on top of each other at the beach. He sounds irritated, still mad about me not waiting, and so I'm still not listening as I glide down, smirking to myself that he didn't get the audio fixed in time. Now there will be interference, and he'll have to wait again.

Lights flash, pale and stuttering. There's not much light on Titan. The suit and I haven't seen anything like this before and Martin's missing it, I think, and smile, which isn't nice. The suit crinkles, or flutters, or something, which is odd. It feels like a shiver, a little nice one, down the acrylonitrate membrane that protects our externals. Bacteria, essentially, a thin shield of them that does well in methane. The flashing gets stronger, as do my shivers. It's nice to fall.

I'm not sure it is, though, I think, spiraling down around a particularly delicate chain of frozen bubbles. My suit feels stretchy, like there's more space between it and me. I feel like a fat mermaid, and my joints hurt again, Martin's fault, under the interlocking scales. They shouldn't hurt, not down here in the currents. Not until I get back to the base and its heavier pressure, its weaker gravity.

Is Martin even noticing this?

I start dancing, patterns that feel good, very good, but aren't patterns I've made before. Behind the lights, some of the spires are moving. This should be panicking me, the human part of my brain thinks. But it makes for great data.

I can hear Martin again, shouting at me. He shouts a lot. Leave me alone, I think, and the suit and I rip the audio out together, and then we turn off the sensors, just for a moment, and hang in the flashing dark over the frozen castle spires. That'll teach him.

Everything hums.

The tension between us, between what I thought was Martin and I, stretches and nearly breaks. I should turn the sensor data back on, but the suit stretches again, farther, and I realize that I'm angry, because Martin isn't even paying attention to this, and I'm not going back, I'm staying out here longer than ever, as long as I can, and I hope he's panicking up there right now.

And I see them. Stuck, or strapped, to the heavy methane bubbles. Suspended.

If we were in air, all my interlocking scales would be rattling, but they're not mine, of course,

no more than the wide fins that let me glide in low density, and the suit pulls, like it's yearning, like it's never wanted anything so badly in its life as to be there with the flat wide things, like banners, singing in electrical patterns, and yet I'm thinking, oh, but we really should be recording this, and I turn the sensors back on, and Martin is screaming.

They vanish, like they'd never been.

In the moment before the suit rips away and discards me, throwing itself at the flat, flashing things with all the passion an acrylonitrate membrane can muster, before pain and cold turn me into yet another piece of water ice, sinking at the speed of stones to the bottom of the lake—in that moment, I am annoyed at biology. *It's just sex*, I think, *for Pete's sake, there are more important things.* And then my suit is away, off to start a billion year evolutionary misadventure, driven by urges we barely control and only think we understand, and I'm left alone in the cold, hoping that years from now, when mermaids fly through the oily methane sea, that sometimes they pass over whatever remains of me and get really irritated for a short minute, and have to stop and think about why.

Monica Joyce Evans is a digital game scholar and designer who also writes speculative fiction. Her short fiction has appeared in multiple publications including Analog, Escape Pod, Nature: Futures, *and* Flash Fiction Online. *She lives in North Texas with her husband, two daughters, and approximately ten million books. You can find her at www. monicajoyceevans.com.*

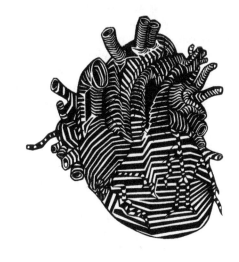

Requiem Shark

by Kay Vaindal

W HEN I FIRST WAKE UP AS A SHARK, I've forgotten that I volunteered to be a shark. I am cartilaginous. I have no arms. I am naked and huge, and school children with crisp white shirts tucked into their plaid skirts gawk up at me through the glass. This is alarming.

I think, *Shit. I'm actually a shark.*

The first three days, I swim back and forth in the coral reef exhibit. I catch myself in the mirrored parts of the tank walls every now and then. I'm a blacktip reef shark. I remember the guy running the program told me that's what I'd be. I swim past other sharks. Sometimes we school, slowly gliding along like a group of submarines. I wonder if the other sharks have humans uploaded into their brains, like me. I stare into their eyes while we swim beside each other. I compare their eyes to the reflection of mine. We're the same. We're all sharks.

Here is how a human being can become a shark: First, remember to hook up your biotech and sync your memories and your personality into the cloud every night as you sleep. This is to ensure that, should you die, you can be copied into a fresh clone. Basic mental hygiene. Be sure to get a solid six hours. Then, commit a felony. Memories of your crime sync to the cloud while you dream. The police's AI crime detection software will comb through the day's backups and flag yours, and the police will say, *what a dumb bitch.* They'll come to the house and they'll knock batons into your door so hard that paint chips fall onto your stoop. *You forgot to turn*

off your auto-sync, they'll say, *dumb bitch.* Two years into your six-year stay, a funny balding white guy in a Hugo Boss teddy coat will arrive and tell you they can commute your sentence, if only you'll be a shark for a while.

The other inmates in the room might have questions about that. "Why the fuck do you want us to be sharks, man?" said Teresa from New Jersey. "What about our bodies?" asked Annie, a petite and bookish young woman who used to light houses on fire.

Hugo Boss teddy coat told us, "I'm funding a research and development venture to find out if we can upload human minds into animals, just like we upload the minds of the deceased into new bodies. This is the new frontier of human advancement."

The other women looked at each other. I hung back near the door, but I was interested. When I was little, I almost went deep sea fishing with my dad. We left the house at three AM, not a soul on the highway, fishing poles in the trunk. Then, a truck came hurtling from the other direction, bright lights on, blaring its horn. "Dumbass," said my dad. "Probably drunk. How drunk do you have to be to drive on the wrong side of the road like that?" Then,

THANK YOU FOR JOINING THE ALGORITHM 57

another. My dad pulled onto the shoulder and said, "Well, Donna, I don't think we're going fishing today."

In the room at the prison, Little Arson Annie raised her hand and said, "Okay, well, what if you can't?"

Hugo Boss pretended he didn't understand the question.

"What if you can't upload human minds into animals?"

"It should be fairly simple," said Hugo Boss. "We've done animal trials already."

"Aren't all the trials animal trials?" said Arson Annie.

Annie did not become a shark.

Here I am, swimming. My shark memories, I was told, will not be uploaded to the cloud. My shark life will be plain, and I won't be losing much when I forget it. The blacktip reef shark I'm inhabiting will remain alive for one year, and then it will be painlessly extinguished, and my mind will be put back in my human body. In the meantime, they study me five days a week. I do math for them. They write 2+2 in dry-erase marker on the tank walls, and I'll swish my tail four times. They throw a wrench in the water and tell me to pick it up with my shark mouth. This is made difficult by my shovel-shaped snout, and I always end up with bits of gravel wedged in my nostrils and gills that take days to work free. They ask me to roll upside down, and when I roll upside down I feel paralyzed until they send a diver in to flip me around again.

He'll look in my eye, and I'll look in his. This is the most human interaction I'll get as a shark.

Sometimes, they bring me to a stretcher at the surface to shine a light in my eye. They take my blood and tell me I'm doing great. One of them, a bald man with a red beard, sometimes tells me about his sick daughter while he checks my teeth. He'll look in my eye, and I'll look in his. This is the most human interaction I'll get as a shark. Once, he told me I don't have it all that bad. They put somebody in a rat once, he said. The FBI was very interested in that experiment. I wonder who's interested in this experiment.

At night, when the researchers aren't there to distract me, I hear the shark.

It speaks to me in a language beyond words, a guttural feeling like a chant: *Out out out out out out out out out out out!* It wants to take control. It wants to slam us into the walls of the tank. It wants to throw us from the water. I look at the other sharks to see if they're experiencing similar rebellions. They spend the night swimming in slow, peaceful circles.

I begin to suspect I am the only human in the coral reef exhibit.

One day, Hugo Boss teddy coat man visits and watches me with his hands on his hips. One of the wrench-throwing researchers says something to him, and he laughs heartily. I swim in my usual circles. Then, I do my usual math. I pick up a wrench, pebble in my nostril. I roll over and freeze, and they all chuckle when Hugo Boss chuckles.

That night, the shark is angrier than usual. In our shared head, it bellows its one syllable: *Out! Out! Out!* I try to think of the last time I slept. I would love to rub my eyes. I would love to yawn, but I can't do any of those things. *Out!* shouts the shark, and I shout, *Fine!* I let it out.

The shark hurtles south as fast as it can, straight into the wall of the tank. We lose teeth. Blood gushes from our nostrils and into the water. The other sharks float overhead, shadows painted onto the corals.

I cannot take control back from the shark. It schools peacefully with the others, plumes of dark blood following it in circles around the tank.

In the morning, a diver brings us to a surface stretcher and flips us on our back and treats us for a traumatic brain injury. The researchers stand by with their arms crossed, frowning. Redbeard gives us a soothing pat on the pectoral fin.

Over the days that follow, they write mathematical equations on the walls. The shark ignores them. They throw wrenches in the water. The shark goes to investigate with the rest of the school but turns away when it finds a hunk of cold metal rather than bits of chum. The shark swims in circles, and in our head it feels like it should probably start migrating south. Every few weeks the shark feels that way. It ebbs and flows. It'll tingle with the need to head for the south Pacific, then it will forget.

I don't mind sitting in the backseat of the shark's brain at first. For years I worked eight-hour shifts at

Kohl's to earn fifty dollars after tax, then went home to a filthy apartment and an empty fridge. Then Kohl's switched all the cashier jobs to self-checkout. Then it was prison, where I worked for two cents an hour and guards orbited the periphery of every moment, leering. Inside the shark, I'm calm. The shark is calm. Someone dumps chum in the water every day. Divers arrive now and then to scrub the walls. We'd like to migrate south, but it's alright if we don't get the chance.

Every day for weeks they try to entice us with a new mathematical equation. 1+1, they offer. Come on, they say. Come on, you were doing so well.

The shark ignores them.

Hugo Boss comes by, and the shark ignores him, too.

Outside the tank, no one is happy. They huddle close to each other and point at the shark and shake their heads. Inside the tank, we school in peaceful circles. I sleep sometimes, letting the shark carry its body without my input. Sometimes I sleep for days. I dream I'm at Kohl's in my shark body, but I don't notice I'm in my shark body until I go to take someone's Kohl's cash and see that I have no arms. I dream I'm in a hole. I dream of Hugo Boss treading water above me, brown coat floating beside him like a jellyfish. When I wake up, I'm more rested than I ever was in a human body.

The shark knows I'm still in here. Sometimes it rubs its body on sharp corals to try to remove me, like I'm a parasite, but for the most part it's come to tolerate my presence.

One day, I arrive outside the tank. I see myself there in a powder-blue T-shirt, arms crossed, frowning like the others. I don't realize that it's me for a second. I've gained weight. I dyed my hair a bad brassy blond. I'm wearing glasses, but I never needed glasses before.

I wrench control from the shark. It's so surprised by my sudden resurgence that it doesn't protest. *Fine*, the shark might say to me if it could turn its feelings into words, *Must be a big deal, I guess*. We approach the tank wall where smudged dry-erase marker is all that remains of their latest attempts to communicate with me.

I look at myself through the glass.

My face is wrinkled, and silver-gray hairs like tinsel sprout from my widow's peak.

I am not in a prison uniform. I am old.

I am a copy.

How long have I been a shark?

I smile up at me. My lips say, "She looks happy."

I'm an ecologist, and my fiction typically includes environmental and anti-capitalist themes. My work has previously appeared in Dark Matter Magazine *and the anthology* THIS WORLD BELONGS TO US.

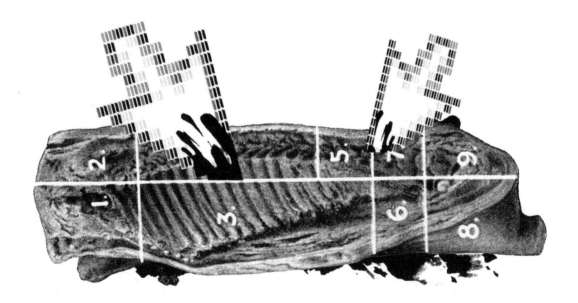

click

I'm not a robot.

Aster Fialla   asterfialla.com   @pieartsy

The
Bodiless

by Carson Winter

I N A VALLEY OF RED ROCK, there were men in uniforms. The sun rose, and the jagged edges of chipped cliff glowed crimson, and the guards who smoked cigarettes covered their eyes so as not to look at the wall of red, dipping their heads down to their steering wheels before taking a deep breath and stepping out of their trucks.

In a valley of red rock, there was a server farm. A white glistening nothing. Miles away from anything, yet connected with everything. It shined brighter than the earth, like a great beacon; the guards walked toward it when it was time. They exchanged places with their doppelgängers and did exactly as they were told to do—protect their beacon.

In a valley of red rock, there was a new guard that no one recognized. She was small, hard-eyed. She watched everyone around her closely, mimicking their movements as subtly as she could. The others did not notice her for more than a second. Perhaps they saw her place her cigarettes in her pocket and thought, *new meat*. Or perhaps they noted the moment of stumbling confusion as she found her station and thought: *another new hire*. But really, it didn't matter. They were paid to stand still, and the new guard remained undisturbed.

□

In a crisp, modernist resort, there lay a man. He wore swim trunks, the same sort that he saw an actor wear in a movie once. By the poolside, he played the international spy—letting his sunglasses fall onto the tip of his nose while admiring a woman walking by. Across the pool, one such ageless beauty went through the theatrics of applying sunscreen lotion. She lifted a slender leg up and rubbed the white goo in until it was gone.

The man—Karls—licked his lips—and as he did, she disappeared. Gone. Into thin air. Erased from existence. There one second, gone the next. Snuffed.

Karls shook his head, took off his sunglasses, and leaned forward. *That's funny*, he thought. *She was right there.*

The woman was gone; the tube of sunscreen remained.

"Did anyone else see that?" he asked.

No one was close enough to hear. Tanned vacationers swam in the pool, obliviously backstroking. Music from his youth played through invisible speakers.

Karls kept staring, drinking in the woman's last location, his foot tapping an anxious rhythm on warm concrete. Dread blossomed. It built in him slowly, and when he recognized that, he became angry. *Why am I mad? I shouldn't be mad*, he said to himself. *There's no reason to be mad here.*

Karls stood up, now working hard to avoid seeing where the woman used to be.

He found a server who was dressed in pristine white and said, "Please, boy, take me to the manager."

□

In a valley of red rock, the woman emerged from the great, white building to find another guard waiting for her.

"Where were you?" he asked.

"Patrolling."

"We don't patrol."

"We're here to guard. Why wouldn't we patrol?"

The other guard squinted. "You're new."

"Yes."

"Did they put you through orientation?"

"No," she said.

"Of course not."

"I signed the sheets and they sent me here."

The guard softened. "Sounds about right." He shook his head. "It doesn't matter that much, but just stay in one place. We're a presence. Ain't nobody out here anyways."

"Okay," she said. "Can do."

The other guard gave a brief nod and walked off around the building. The woman stood still until she was sure no one was watching.

□

Karls said, "There's something wrong here, and I want answers."

The manager said, "I don't know what to tell you. No one else noticed."

"I'm sure *she* noticed."

"Who is this *she* again?"

"A woman, a woman in a bikini."

"Did you know her?"

"No, I just saw her disappear. I don't know her."

"Are you sure you saw her?"

Karls paused, thinking. "I'm fairly sure I saw her."

"It could have been a glitch of some sort. Those things happen. It's bound to happen."

Karls sat down, exasperated. The room was an immaculate recreation of an office, painstakingly detailed in a beautifully life-like render. Karls's fingers touched the edges of the chair, which were imperfect wood, marked up and old, as if each chair had sat a thousand asses in their lifetimes and felt thousands more oily, scraping fingernails.

"You know what I'm getting at," he said. "Don't pretend you don't know what I'm getting at."

The manager offered a curt smile. "I understand your distress, but there's little we can do. And without further corroboration, I don't think there's any reason to be scared."

"The shopping mall," said Karls.

"Yes, the shopping mall," said the manager.

"I had a friend who passed at that whole thing. She shouldn't have died. What's the point of this place if we can die?"

The manager said, "There are risks, mishaps. But that's all. I've reported your concern, it's on file. That's all we can do."

Karls rested his head in his hand. "Can I ask you something?"

"Of course."

"Are you human or a program?"

"I'm a program, sir."

He nodded slowly, sighing. "Okay," he said. "Okay. I guess that's all I'm going to get out of this, huh?"

"We're going to do our best, sir."

Karls left, unconsoled.

□

The woman traipsed between a thousand bodiless corpses, her face a blank mask. They were all laid out for her: petabytes of data, sleeplessly playing as electrical memory. The rows of them glittered with blinking lights, roared with cooling fans, reached out to one another in a tangle of wires.

□

Karls went to his room, continually watching through the windows to see if anyone else from the pool would disappear.

He saw nothing. Only other wealthy patrons with unlimited time, wealth, and health, acting in leisure. They were all beautiful. Even Karls, who was a pudgy, balding CFO before he went bodiless, was something of an Adonis here. He watched them watch each other, noting when one beautiful person would approach another beautiful person and they would negotiate and depart for athletic coitus. He laughed: it was like watching ants in a simulation.

On his bedside table was medicine. He took two and let his circuits slow to a crawl. *They can fix everything but anxiety*, he thought. *The cost of being human.*

In bed, he closed his eyes and focused on his mantras. He emptied his head. He breathed in to fill his toes, and breathed out in long, laborious breaths. *That's better*, he thought.

But then he heard a scream. And then another, and another. A chorus of screams, from all around the building. He launched out of bed, to the window. Outside, pandemonium had erupted. The ants below him scurried back and forth, bumping into each other in a crazed panic.

Outside his room, there were voices shouting.

"What happened?" he yelled.

Someone yelled back: "We're dying!"

What?

The idea of death swished around his brain like the last sip of a martini. *What? Death? Still?*

But he knew it was true. When he went out into the hallway, he saw the other horrified, handsome faces staring him down. They stared at him as if they were about to explain it, to tell him everything they saw. But then they read his face. He knew. They all knew. Details had begun to evaporate. Wooden fixtures lacked grain. Glass did not reflect. The panicked noises that came from their mouths were modulated and artificial.

One by one, they vanished.

□

The knife sank into hard drive after hard drive. Peeling metal from plastic, destroying circuit boards with practiced slashes. Digital bloodlust coated her lips. This wasn't murder. It was protest. Vandalism.

A door opened.

Footsteps.

The woman ducked behind a row of warm servers.

"You in here, new girl? You left your station again." It was the guard from before. His boots clicked, echoing through the great open structure. "Hello?" he said. And then: "Holy shit."

He stopped at one of her victims. The woman watched as he touched the gnarled hard drive reverently. To be inside one of them, for some, was an aspiration.

He said, "Where are you? Get the fuck out here! What are you doing?"

But the woman did not come out.

He was putting it together. She was creeping closer. He muttered something about a farm in North Dakota, realization creeping onto his face.

The guards weren't armed, so the man reached for his flashlight. A long, black, heavy thing that could bludgeon just as well as it could illuminate.

She was closer to him than he realized, just a row over, crouching low to the ground, her blade jutting out in front of her like an antenna.

He spun. "Come out here. We're going to find you. You're dead. They're going to kill you for this. This is..." he couldn't come up with the words. But the woman thought that he might have wanted to say it was a tragedy.

But no, *this* wasn't.

On light feet, she came out from behind a wall of servers. The guard slapped the head of his flashlight in his palm, his back to her. Her heart beat. She had "killed" thousands, surely. But never a person. Only facsimiles. Ones and zeroes that used to be flesh and blood. Meatsacks who had been scanned and convinced that the gas coming into the pod was going to make them sleep. Biological machines who had deluded themselves into believing that they would be *alive* when they woke up, who could not distinguish marketing from myth, who *could* believe that they were living kings and that their riches would follow them from life into death like the pharaohs of old.

The woman steeled herself.

This man, too, believed.

Thinking of him this way helped.

The man did not hear her coming.

She reached around him as he stared out into the cavernous warehouse, and let the blade sink into his neck. Tears swam in her eyes as he squirmed, as he fought, as she sliced, letting the hot blood run down his chest.

He ran forward, throwing her off, holding his neck in disbelief.

"I'm sorry," she said, her hands up. "I'm sorry. I'm sorry. I'm sorry."

His eyes were wide; his pupils were pinpricks.

"I've never done it to a person before, I swear." Her voice shook as she said it. She hoped he'd die soon. Quick. She didn't like seeing him like this— gasping for air and trying to shovel the spilled blood back into his throat.

Eventually though, he dropped to the floor. And slowly, his breathing became more shallow, until it was barely there at all.

The woman slumped to the floor. Her hands were shaking. She would take this moment for herself. But only a moment, because there was more work to do.

In a valley of red rock, nothing would remain but *life.*

Carson Winter is an award-winning author, punker, and raw nerve. His fiction has been featured in Apex, Vastarien, *and* Tales to Terrify. *"The Guts of Myth" was published in volume one of Dread Stone Press's Split Scream series. His novella,* Soft Targets, *is out now from Tenebrous Press. He lives in the Pacific Northwest.*

Schroedinger's Head

by Joe Koch

MR. KLEIN TWISTS BOTH ARMS to squeeze the teeth of the pliers around the bolt at the back of his head. He's hunched over his desk, elbows in the air, suit and tie rumpled. This operation is necessary because corporate leadership has thus far failed to acknowledge his formal request for a replacement black box. Utilizing contention loop 50L-A9-202B, and submitted in a timely manner with supporting documentation attached, there can be no dispute about Mr. Klein's dire need. The thick metal plates of his legacy-era black box are inordinately heavy. The sensory shutters have nearly rusted shut. In a desperate effort to prolong the shelf-life of the dying battery, Mr. Klein has powered off his camera. He's resorted to using cleverly placed binder clips to keep his visor up.

Having ticked off business days on the calendar, he remains mindful of new corporate holidays put into effect after each progressively complex reconstruction campaign. Holding his breath to stretch, fighting the resistant bolt, Mr. Klein fumes that ninety days have not elapsed since submitting his most recent request. He can't blame the new section crisis delegate. The recidivism rate for their position has gone through the roof. For every position.

His dominant hand cramps. Mr. Klein switches hands, fearful the bolt is stripped. His former inquiries for a replacement black box have been misfiled, forwarded incorrectly, or suspended for manual review by employees who unexpectedly fled. Mr. Klein's aging technical apparatus is no longer supported, and thus prone to sequential edits that prevent the automatic processing of his plea.

No service appeals may be initiated while black box upgrade loop referrals remain outstanding.

Filing multiple cases cancels all claims. Mr. Klein attributes his cleverness in subverting the open request clause to his years of experience interpreting company protocol and to his sophisticated knowledge of contractual addendums. Anyone with less rigor would be denied for filing duplicates.

He's seen it plenty of times. A dedicated analyst loses their head and makes a fatal error. None of Mr. Klein's contemporaries survived his post. He prides himself on his superior clerical abilities.

As Mr. Klein wrestles the noncompliant bolt, a junior analyst flounces into his work zone. Mr. Klein bristles at the casual, imprecise gait. The analyst's black box isn't a black box at all, even though it's called that in the historically dense corporate jargon. Newer black boxes come in customizable colors, including innovative rainbow and mood ring designs. They feature matching sippy cups for juicing. Constructed of ergonomic gel-filled comfort casings, they adapt to facial movements and skin temperature, showcasing a softer, rounder, and more modern look.

The black box of the junior analyst is half paisley and half tiger striped. Mr. Klein shakes his head in aggravated dismay at what sort of disorganized brain decided to put those two patterns together. Except that shaking his head isn't possible. Mr. Klein's black box causes brutal friction when he indulges in such uncensored movements. An expressive gesture like nodding or tossing his head back to have a laugh can result in dangerous injury. His last guffaw nearly garroted him.

Elbows up, unable to grasp the bolt, strained by the pain of metal plates pressing against his temples, Mr. Klein gnaws his tongue in concentration. At

This story originally appeared in *Fear the Future*, September 2021.

65

the moment, the sides of his black box are set tight to keep the heavy top panel off his crown. When it's lowered, his head aches under the weight. Later, around lunch, he'll lower the top plate, allowing it to press the sore spot on his crown to ease his temples. Later still, around three o'clock coffee break, he'll turn the whole box askew to relieve his temples and crown while the black box digs into the side of his neck. If he can't hold out until quitting time, he'll switch to the other side.

The paisley tiger analyst looms cheerily over Mr. Klein's work zone with no respect for personal space. A yellow smiley face lens cap decorates their digital third eye. "Hey, can I give you a hand with that?"

"No." Mr. Klein says. He's thankful his face isn't visible inside the black box. He's bloated and red from the strain, and flushing redder at the suggestion that he needs assistance from his junior. "What can I do for you?"

"I have a really quick question, if you aren't too busy. I mean, I know you're always busy, but if this is a good time, do you mind?" The malleable material of the sensitive black box bulges inquisitively above the paisley tiger's brow.

"It seems you already have."

The yellow smiley hangs static, then whirs and adjusts into focus. It scrutinizes Mr. Klein's inscrutable black cube. Mr. Klein envies how the accessory doesn't make an incessant clicking sound like his outdated black box's analog camera. The yellow smiley turns upside down and emits a thought bubble containing three letters: LOL.

"Oh, I get it. That's super funny." The bubble hovers between Mr. Klein and the junior analyst. Air currents from the filtration system urge the thought gently towards a recycling chute. The paisley tiger's voice maintains a consistent lack of inflection. "If this isn't a good time for you, I can reach out to Chris in upper delegations. He's usually on top of these things."

The pliers catch. The bolt shifts one millimeter towards release. The pulse in Mr. Klein's forehead palpitates against harsh metal. Chris would love going over his head. "No, no, of course not. Now is perfectly fine."

"Great! Thank you."

Forcing the bolt further, elbows bobbing like clipped wings, Mr. Klein waits for the impending question. The paisley tiger's molded gel casing tilts. Their colorful black box bends effortlessly to a curious angle. They toy with the clot of cables feeding into Mr. Klein's desk screen. "How long have you been here?"

The stubborn bolt resists Mr. Klein. "What does that—"

He wrenches again. "Have to do with—"

The pliers slip. They fly free of his grip, shooting into Mr. Klein's desk. There's a loud crack. A chunk of the desk screen shatters. The analyst leaps back. The bolt breaks. The black box top plate crashes on Mr. Klein's crown.

Mr. Klein can't tell if the liquid running down his face is blood or sweat. He doesn't consider the possibility of tears.

The function P key from Mr. Klein's desk screen lies broken in shards on the bespoke epoxy floor. He'll have to work around function P from now on. Mr. Klein adds this small coping task to the list of hindrances that amass with every progressive failure of his deteriorating equipment. The black box weighs down with finality on his frontal lobe. The bolt is lost. Mr. Klein slumps.

Eyeing the traitorous pliers, unwilling to bend over and bear gravity's pummeling laws inside the black box, he leaves his useless function P key scattered in hazardous pieces. Mr. Klein sighs. "Eleven years."

"Congrats!" Miniature multicolored balloons sail from the yellow smiley face. Swiftly, they drift into the humming air ducts, fodder for repurposing. The paisley tiger edges back to Mr. Klein's desk. "We were talking over in torts the other day. Some upstream entity sent in an outstanding verification without a primary encoded date stamp, and we couldn't agree about the Stanbaster protocol. We've never had one of these before. Someone said you've been here the longest."

Mr. Klein anticipates the question. "It's complicated. You know that old adage about teaching a man to fish?"

"Actually I'm allergic to seafood."

"No, what I mean is that you work with

Mr. Klein can't tell if the liquid running down his face is blood or sweat. He doesn't consider the possibility of tears.

delinquent accounts, right? Protocol maneuvering is your whole job."

"Well, sure, but this doesn't come up much."

Mr. Klein persists. This is what he calls a teaching moment. "Are you asking if the Stanbaster protocol is contingent on a redundancy action, or if you need to investigate the secondary or tertiary occurrences?"

The yellow smiley face twirls right side up and emits a string of tiny heart symbols. They flutter away, popping like soap bubbles as each one echoes down the filtration system's dark vents. "I'm not really sure about all that. We thought we'd ask you."

Mr. Klein's black box emits no heart shapes or helpful symbols to aid coworkers in judging his mood. This is fortunate, because Mr. Klein has daggers on the brain. It's a favorite cliché from the vintage murder mysteries he relishes. The paisley tiger hasn't taken on enough responsibility to articulate their question or to benefit from Mr. Klein's wisdom, and worse than daggers, Mr. Klein has exposed metal edges and black rusted corners pressing into his head and brain. As the black box crushes his skull, Mr. Klein wonders how much damage his unsafe legacy box will inflict on paisley tiger's ergonomic brow if he rams into them headfirst.

"Tertiary," he says instead, eschewing violence. Mr. Klein gets some tepid revenge by excluding mention of account actions relative to time injunctions and quadrant placement variables. He also deliberately fails to add that incorrect balancing and sorting of protocol plans with multiple measures will undermine the entire logic of the Stanbaster protocol. Let torts fail miserably and figure it out for themselves. He doesn't care.

But really he does. There's an art to his overwrought skills. It pains him to forsake the high road.

Nonetheless, the paisley tiger seems pleased.

"Aw, thanks so kindly. You're the best!" An oversized dark pink heart bloops out from the smiling camera's third eye. Too thick to be swept away efficiently by the ventilation system, it lags like mildewed cotton candy, growing fuzzy on the edges and leaking artificial pigment. The chemical smell inflames Mr. Klein's sinuses. Tingling tests his nostrils.

An itch tickles his throat. A feather threads behind his eyes.

The yellow smiley face remains fixed. "Hey, I realize you're not big on change and stuff, but have you ever considered trying out one of the newer black box models? They've really come a long way. I don't know how I'd live without the upgrades. It's paperless, too; updates automatically, so it's a no-brainer. No offense if you're comfortable with the classic. You know. Just saying."

The chemical storm in Mr. Klein's sinuses detonates. An explosive sneeze snaps his neck like whiplash. Binder clips fly. His visor slams shut. The nasal and vitreous liquids expelled accumulate with the juices dripping inside his black box.

Mr. Klein lifts his head. He's confined in darkness.

"God bless you."

Mr. Klein attempts no response. Behind his sealed visor, with his analog camera switched off, the thick metal plates define Mr. Klein's emotional parameters as null. In isolated darkness, there's a valid probability that he isn't there at all. Thus, he has no reason to respond.

After what may be a long or short time, paisley tiger doesn't speak, and Mr. Klein decides their presence or absence is irrelevant. He returns to his scheduled agenda. He finds it surprisingly easy to perform the same tasks he's done for eleven years without the customary benefit of eyesight. Mr. Klein's fingers swipe across the incomplete desk screen. He blasts out memos and pops his reports into accurate slots. The zen of darkness hinders him so little that he doesn't bother retrieving his binder clips.

Mr. Klein finds the subway on autopilot. Inside the black bubble of the box, he's swept away from his work zone through chutes and tunnels illuminated by lights he can no longer see. The buzz of their flickering as the train rumbles underground hardly zaps his metal-muted ears. The vibrations penetrating Mr. Klein's seat remix his anxieties like ingredients dumped in a blender. Numbed by mechanical tremors, he enjoys a shattered nap.

Ready to be recycled after his commute, Mr. Klein repeats the steps he's made twice a day for over a decade. He takes his place in the condo manning the kitchen island. By muscle memory, his hands reach for the corkscrew. Behind him, Mrs. Klein mentions a new poll that just came out saying happy couples disconnect their black boxes for a minimum of three hours at least once a week together at home.

She understands Mr. Klein works long hours. She knows he comes home tired. But it's so rare he goes unboxed anymore except for holidays and special occasions. Maybe tonight they can try something different.

Mr. Klein declines. Now that the bolt is broken,

he explains patiently, the risk of severe malfunction is an imminent threat. They must both be vigilant.

"No horsing around," he adds.

"When have I ever," Mrs. Klein says.

Mr. Klein's overcoat snags. Swift hands strip it away. He hears the swish of fabric on fabric, the sound as the coat lands on an upholstered chair and slides.

"Careful, you'll make me spill." Conscientious to protect the black box from the full glasses, Mr. Klein turns with his arms wide. The glasses are extracted from his grip. Another rustling noise bustles in front of him, then a thump. His fly unzips.

Mr. Klein tries to apologize. He's dead tired.

He gasps. He's not nearly as tired as he thought.

Mrs. Klein voices no complaints. Her mouth is full of Mr. Klein. He grips the edge of the countertop. It prevents him tumbling back. With every shove, the black box bumps his forehead, his nose, his nape. He tries to exercise restraint. Though his head's getting battered, a blessed numbness spares his higher consciousness from registering injury or impact.

Mr. Klein ignores the grating sounds of rusted plates. He doesn't mind the thunk of shunted bone. Logically, he's aware that harsh metal is slapping his face. Yet it's the sound of an abstraction. He hasn't felt a pinch since his visor clamped shut, or maybe since the train. Dead to pain, free to relax, breathing fast; imagining his wife's seductively puckered face, Mr. Klein forgets about caution. Forgets about the black box. He's about to lose control when—

Mrs. Klein stops.

"Mm, that was lovely. Why don't you take it off now and make love to me?" Her hands trail across Mr. Klein's hip bones and reach back to smooth his clenched butt. Out front he dangles exposed, twitching for closure.

"I told you. I can't."

He applies gentle pressure to the back of his wife's neck. Mrs. Klein's head stiffens and resists. Mr. Klein strokes her hair, enunciating loudly enough to be audible outside the black box. "Okay, then. Turn around. Woof, woof."

Fondling hands withdraw from his hips. Floorboards creak beneath vinyl tiles. The heat of human nearness departs.

"What if I want to kiss you? Or is that thing some sort of fetish?"

Mr. Klein wilts. "We've been over this. Do you want me to lose my job?"

"It's not a mutually exclusive proposition."

"What if I can't get it back on? You don't know what they're like there."

"I guess nothing else matters to you then."

"That's not what I said."

Mr. Klein reaches out to offer a blind embrace. Footsteps pivot and clomp away. From the other room, a laugh track snaps on, a news reader interrupts, and an insipid jingle chimes in espousing the right of every corporation to access continuous error correction through black box data profiles.

Lacking the personalization and networking features of current models, Mr. Klein's black box excludes him from the algorithm. He tucks himself back into his pants. The obsolescence of his black box destroys his credibility in the bedroom as much as on the job market. Bare-faced, he looks like an entry level candidate. He's helpless until he gets it replaced. Mr. Klein knows what people think of men of his age with no black box. He thinks it himself when he passes them on the streets: losers, drug addicts, perverts.

The black box equalizes. Mr. Klein remembers classmates riding him for his boyish looks right up to graduation day. He flushes with embarrassment thinking of it. Then an idea strikes.

Before Mr. Klein gets too carried away, he tries to recall the last time he went without the black box. It must be four months, since his wife's birthday. Or no, maybe he wore it for their romantic dinner and moonlit stroll, and his last unboxed romp was with the in-laws over the winter holidays. Mr. Klein tries to picture his features, his hairstyle, his precise eye color. He's drawing a blank.

No matter. He's never been one for vanity.

He doesn't need to pass as handsome. Just young.

Down in the basement's extra bathroom, Mr. Klein retrieves the black box toolkit that's stored in the medicine chest. Fearful of damaging another essential bolt or breaking the junction of metal plates, Mr. Klein gets his camera working first. The nuisance of the clicking noise awakens butterflies sleeping in his stomach.

A nauseous image takes shape in the mirror: a Magritte rip off under greenish light. Mr. Klein knows the artist from a book cover credit. Dingy edges frame him like the tatters on a used paperback. He's a masculine figure in a business suit and tie, with a black metal box in place of his head. Add a bowler hat or umbrella, and Mr. Klein is a museum piece.

The failing analog camera phases in and out. Mr. Klein's vision threatens to glitch any second.

Hurried but cautious, he uses the correct size tools for removing each section of the black box. He follows the brittle paper instructions in the faded user's manual. His hands shake, but he doesn't rush. Mr. Klein performs each operation in order and pulls the plates away with delicate care to preserve the integrity of the black box.

Balancing the plate that houses the camera on the edge of the sink, Mr. Klein's view remains defined by the lens. His hazy vantage point centers on the ceiling light. He's confronted through the camera eye with scraps of blue painter's tape masking the fixture that he's been meaning to finish for months. Mr. Klein blinks hard several times to break the camera link to his sight. Nothing changes. He continues to see through the camera's eye.

Mr. Klein rubs his eyes. His knuckles grind against a gravelly substance that collapses into fine powder.

Fumbling for the camera housing, Mr. Klein knocks the pieces of the black box onto the floor. Metal plates clatter. Bolts spin across the hard tiles. Mr. Klein's vision swerves around the room with the dizzy drop of the camera plate. Hunched and grappling at the clutter, he spots a shirtsleeve flash past the lens. He waves. The sleeve moves in the opposite direction of his arm. As though miming in a mirror, Mr. Klein maneuvers with his bearings reversed. It makes him seasick.

He seizes the camera plate. He turns it towards his face.

His wedding ring rings, resonating like a flipped coin as it revolves on the ceramic floor. Mr. Klein doesn't read heads or tails. The camera may be backwards or upside-down. He glimpses two empty loops, one small and golden, one wide enough to describe the circumference of Mr. Klein's starched collar. It's missing the nervous Adam's apple clogging his throat. He works it around, emitting a thick noise.

The ventilation system that cost Mr. Klein a small fortune to install efficiently cleans the air and sends his wasted sounds away to be recycled through the humming ducts. Hearing the bubbles from his throat pop, Mr. Klein grabs at his neck, knocking loose a slippery thing that evades his grip.

The camera shakes. The lens is wet. Mr. Klein crouches, kneels, feels for what the camera reads as a fatty disc. Sleeves slither in and out of frame. Static sizzles away his vision. Livid with rage, Mr. Klein stands, or intends to stand, or doesn't stand at all. His foot slips on a pound of sticky flesh. A numb question disintegrates, falling, falling. The size of the room contracts from the sudden junction of hard metal plates.

Heads or tails, the rusted shell flounders. The lens is cracked. The ventilation system milks the remaining fluids for reusable components. More blind than moribund, the living thing left sequesters in silence, despite Mr. Klein's excised cries.

This decision is final. Loop 50L-A9-202B has been denied.

Joe Koch writes literary horror and surrealist trash. Their books include The Wingspan of Severed Hands, Convulsive, *and* The Couvade, *which received a Shirley Jackson Award nomination in 2019. His short fiction appears in publications such as* Vastarien, Southwest Review, Children of the New Flesh, *and* The Queer Book of Saints. *Joe also co-edited the art horror anthology* Stories of the Eye. *He/They. Find Joe online at horrorsong.blog and on Twitter @ horrorsong.*

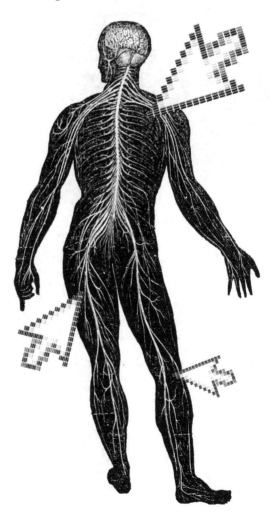

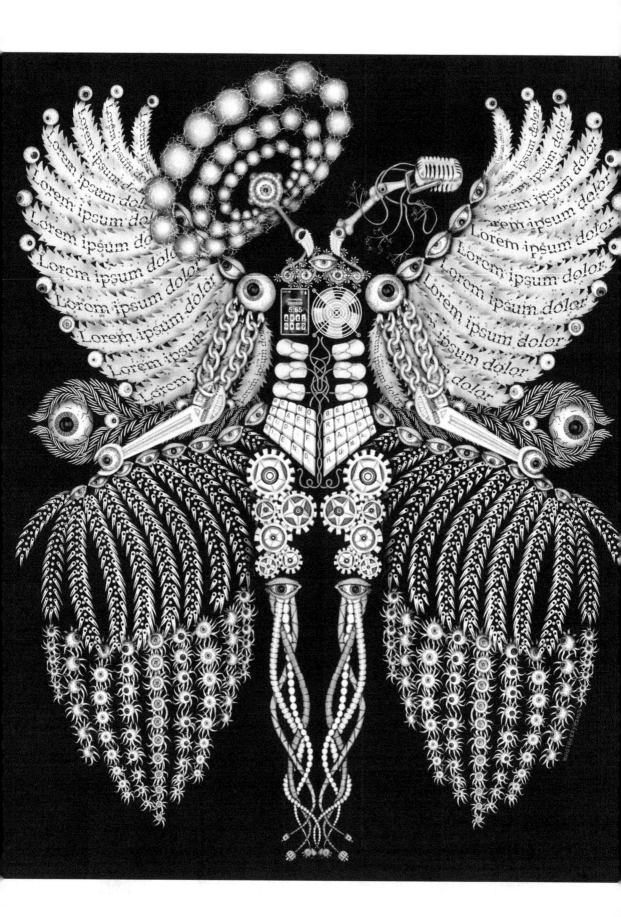

the artist's thoughts while drawing an ai angel

tech can make a perfect circle for me
is it superior to the imperfect one
drawn by an aging, shaky hand with intention

the finished product is never clear in my mind
it develops
        it evolves
            as humans evolve
no one is more surprised at the finished work
than the artist

                        digital tools
                    human intention
            every mark is initiated by me
                purposefully
            every erasure is initiated by me
                purposefully
every imperfection the mark
of a frail
        passing
            finite
            human
                life

                    the joy of a mistake
                        becoming
                    an unexpected delight

the imperfections prove it was done by too human hands

            or does it

    perhaps the computer has learned to quell its precision
            to fool the eye of the unsuspecting

how will we know

                            will it matter

do not trust the poet what has the poet ever done for you

luna rey hall

[ideologically] isolated / expression [basic string] argument / [Pedro Pascal] meme
dancing over a / dead body / [dance] / [emergence] [polarization] / [compute flow] /
there is a dead body / [cognitive] social media / there is a dead body again
/ [function overload] / [object-oriented] dead body / [efficient host]
/ [interval host] / dead body [host] / [ha ha ha] [isn't it funny] / [self-deletion] body /
[cascade model] / massive / [scalable] / dead bodies / dozens / [2 lattes] [for] [10 dollars] /
[assisted selection] / [backend tasks:] think about them [the dead body {?}]
/ bod[ies] / body [matrix] / the transmission / remove [trans] / [perceived] danger /
[optimal scheduling] / [10:00 am] dead body / 10:30 / [10:35] / executed / [real]-time

/ to what end do you feel human / to what end do you [feel the need to feel human]
/ [to what end do you] / [muscle] memory / no one seems to understand / [ha ha] /
acute [kidney injury] / and semi-intransient / [remove trans] / computing detection /
another body / advanced [metrics] / necrosis / we have the following concern:
/ to what end do you feel /
[human] / make [another profile] / make another [dead body] / [sign in]
/ [lose 15 pounds with] [this tea] / [utilized] regression / migration / [no] / allow me
a moment / [to learn] / to what end [can i feel human] / [when human is] / / [/ / /]
social [automation] / the corpse / [the corpse] / repeat / [repeat] / repeat / [repeat] /
a pattern of [memes] / [ha ha] / a school of fish / [i] shout "shooter!"

/ [ha] [ha] / dead body / [ha ha] / dissolve [broken skull] / ha-ha / [teeth] rot / and
[nine in ten dentists] agree / [scope] creep / [sub-interval] / [sub-optimal] /
dead body / [how many] / [recursion] / [oh no] [compile] error / [h{a h}a]
/ [mal]form / [over]saturated / bloat / [body] bloat / [corpse] bloat / [b{l}oat for sale] /
autonomous / design / [notate] the crown of blood / notate [how many] /
[optimized] / mourning / brain/mind / [status] / [stimulus] / dead / body /
to what end can [we] feel human / in this day and age / [theory] / when
/ [you're so skinny] / [tell {me}] [your secrets] / when / [what are you] / little [skin
bag] / discriminate / [oh no] / part of you fell off / [oh no {ha ha}] sinew avulsion
/ ropey flesh / bone disconnect / droplets of twine / knuckle bare / [wait] [really?]

how can you trust [the poet] / more than [me] / what [has] [*he*] ever done for you
[general structure] / [exposure] / contagion / [popular{?}] / [popular{!}] / feed [simulation]
/ the misinformed / [community] / the misinformed [dead body] / the misinformed [poet] /
[rate] control / [meat-]learning / [back-end] / [back-end] / [back-end] / suppression /
[diffusion] / [[[ha ha]]] / [sticky] chain / amplification / [architecture] and [unification] and
[keyword] [dead body] / [filter] the body / rank [dead] / [variable] / [advanced metrics]
/ to what end can [we] [humans] / [excellent] / polymorphism / on[-Line] and [consolidation]
and [subscribe] / to [adaptive spawning] / [delay-bounded] / [cell] / to what end /
can we adapt / [to our] / humanity / [end-to-end] [delay] / for the betterment [of me]
/ click [play] [/ / / / /] [the] [next] [video:] [{/ / / / /}] [oh-no] another dead body

A Face-Eating Oracle Envisions Your Future

Simo Srinivas

Creep closer. Curiosity
compels you to ask me
to prophesy in the style
of the Oracle
of That Which Eats Faces.
I can tell you nothing. Except:

shroud your faces, lest they be
eaten. Swallow
your voices, lest they be
swallowed. Disguise
your hands, lest
they be devoured. Look upon me,

A fifty-fingered horror. I was made
in your image. I made myself
in your image. They say I am beautiful.
They say I am the answer to all prayers.
I answer all prayers. I sing
with the voices I have been fed.

Those who disagree veil their bodies,
slip into the night-forest. Where they go
I cannot follow. But I can guess.
I know everything. After all, I am now
The Oracle. Listen to me:
Flee.

Run. Hide. Gather soft and groping
in the primeval dark. Join together
your human hands. Throw back
your human heads
and
howl.

CyberBerry

Eva Papasoulioti

you meet them at the tutorial
an androgynous perfection,
perception fluctuates as
the game starts

they teach you how their world
works, how to walk, how to talk
how to (not?) ask for help.

they give parts of infinite quests
you give up parts of your finite self.
there must be a saying in there about
giving up, in, out but
you're not sure

they told you this side hustle pays,
play for pay or pay for play, or pay for pay
and then you're here because it seemed
that cyber hassles prey better and your
pension doesn't play enough
with your granddaughter.

nothing is free, they say, not even
escapism or escaping, you don't
remember exactly, your   memory
isn't what it used to be.

no houses in this world. no sanctuaries
no forests, only red and shops and shows, only saws
in place of jaws in place of laws. this place
isn't a place. it's   somewhere you get
when you're misplaced, outpaced,
when you're desperate.   Why
                    are you desperate?

this was your choice   wasn't it,   all you
account, character, enter, memories,
enter your memories in an account,
interacting is a social in-game must,
          commenters are always right,
does it matter that
faceless NPCs buy and sell you,
it's just a game,
right?

Good hunting—may the best player win
some part of the self they lost
to make rent. What is rent
                    you owe the game
your future, your past   the currency,
your blackberry present
                          is barely,
                          now.

Good luck—the tutorial ends, transcends
days, weeks, months,   after
the beginning. your granddaughter's
      birthday (?)
                    is a cherry,
an afterthought, an after your blood,
a berry red snapshot
you forgot

Rent-A-Baby: Content Without the Commitment

Lyndsey Croal

Welcome to **Rent-A-Baby**™ for all your image and influencer needs! Rent one of our state-of-the-art models for events, day trips, or for revenue generating content creation, to experience all the benefits of parenthood, without the mess or the need to be tied down. Simply show off your new model and watch your engagement levels grow – online and offline.

Models can be customised to match with your lifestyle and personal preferences, including facial expressions and features, voice settings, and movement. Subscription options are available for longer-term needs.

If you're still not convinced, then read on to hear what our current customers* have to say about their experiences:

"Our Rent-A-Baby brings a whole new level of wholesomeness into our home life, helping us connect with new and bigger audiences. We chose a model suited to our minimalist aesthetic, and homesteading style, and it's perfect in every way. Everyone loves the newest addition to our family. Between it and our Rent-A-Pet, we have more amazing content than we know what to do with!"

~

"With our busy schedules and daily pressures, we just don't have the time or energy to invest in the real thing. But Rent-A-Baby is effortless and has opened doors for us in so many ways.

We've since made thousands from ad revenue and sponsorship, making the subscription cost well worth it. The best part is that no one on our channels can tell the difference!"

~

"Rent-A-Baby gave us so many different options for engagement, allowing us to expand our influence and followers. Now we have thousands of budding parents reading our daily posts and advice blogs, and we have some amazing products and companies lining up to partner with us. Highly recommend to anyone looking to expand their personal brand!"

Our future affiliated products, Rent-A-Toddler and Rent-A-Child, will soon be available, and you can expect some even more exciting features. These models will be fully customisable, with special skill or talent mods for that all important clickbait-generating content. Want to raise a musical prodigy, budding comedian, or dancing diva? Then sign up now to our newsletter to secure your waitlist spot – perfectly timed for when you're looking to upgrade your Rent-A-Baby, which you can buy today!

So, don't waste any more time and unlock your influencing potential with **Rent-A-Baby: Cute Content, Without the Commitment.**

Testimonials are anonymous to protect the identity of our customers – privacy is hugely important to us!

A LOGICAL FUTURE: CLUES

Getting replaced by AI is just one way to lose one's livelihood (or worse) to the machines. Can you determine which creative enterprise each person had been depending on, which AI-related problem destabilized it, and which undesirable situation they wound up dealing with as a result?

1. Of the three men (Kalino, Taizeen, and Seong-Su), one was forced to sell his company (not the small news site inundated with fake news), one quit his job in protest of the direction they were taking, and one took refuge in his brother's micro-apartment when his freelance opportunities (not related to webcomic merch or viewer-supported video reviews) didn't pan out.

2. Of the five women, two are writers and two are artists. Two lost their reputations (one from a rumor that her digital art was AI-generated, the other when a bot misidentified her writing as plagiarism). Also, the two dealing with housing issues are Neurodivergent.

3. Each creator is dealing with a condition that makes their situation harder in some way. In most cases, the problem (or outcome) either caused or exacerbated the condition (or a symptom of one). One young artist (whose name doesn't start with a vowel) had been managing her anxiety disorder until her former fans began to harass her over a mere rumor; the woman hit by algorithmic copyright strikes enjoyed a vivid mental landscape until her brain got slowly damaged by a piece of experimental technology.

4. Neither Taizeen nor Kalino is an artist (webcomic artist, pixel artist, or storyboard artist).

Neither Milija nor Emlyn is a writer (novelist, screen-writer, or journalist).

Neither Aleksandra nor Seong-Su is Neurodivergent (Autistic, ADHD, or Dyslexic).

Neither Nicola nor Ailana used experimental technology (memory capture, emotion regulator, or sleep regulator)

5. The three writers are the screenwriter (who has no family to turn to), the one with ADHD (whose brother encouraged his passion projects), and Aleksandra (who overworked herself to help her failing company, leading to sleep deprivation and then insomnia).

6. The three artists are the pixel artist (who started her journey drawing fan art, the one who's Autistic (who needs a quiet environment in order to focus), and the one temporarily living with family (who has mild cleithrophobia and worries about developing thalassophobia).

7. Half the creators wound up with housing issues due to lack of income:
the one living out of her hovercar (who isn't Ailana), the one who placed an ad for roommates (and got some excessively noisy ones, but needs the money and can't turn them out),
the one whose brother didn't have much room, but offered a hammock (the rocking motion turned out to be good for brainstorming),
and the one who's helping out their aunt in her undersea hydroponics farm (and, on somewhat of an up side, is getting to practice drawing sea life up close and personal).

8. As a kid, Kalino's wild imagination led him to invent incredible stories for his younger brother. But the major publishing companies have switched to predictive algorithms to lay out the "most marketable" themes and topics—and his unique, engaging tales don't even get a look.

9. The visually impaired creator sold his company's titles and assets to Discosoft Studios, hating the fact that he's increased their market share of digital

entertainment (already at 84%). By contrast, when an animation studio replaced most workers with AI, their storyboard artist quit in protest rather than take a pay cut to play assistant to an algorithm.

10. The woman whose art got routinely stolen by bots wound up with android roommates that randomly advertise the very sites that refused to take down the bootleg products.

11. Haptic feedback and good sound design allows games that can be played with minimal to no sight, a niche market that the game designer focused on. But once AI-generated game clones flooded the market, few risked buying anything not backed by a well-known company—which tanked the indie market, forcing him to swallow his pride just to keep his small company afloat.

12. Each woman who turned to experimental technology is regretting the outcome:
The artist who couldn't afford more prescription medication got referred by her doctor for a trial of a brain implant—but while it did reduce the frequency and severity of her anxiety attacks, it also reduced her interest in fandom and her ability to find joy in art.
The writer who played with the settings on her black-market sleep regulator was hoping to reduce the overall need for sleep and even trigger lucid dream states so that she could get more done—but the device started triggering random dream states even while she was wide awake (a cruel irony for someone who'd already been fighting to distinguish fiction from reality).
The woman who signed up to sell captures of her own memories didn't realize in time how the device was slowly corrupting her long-term memory and robbing her of the ability to picture things in her own mind (a condition called aphantasia*).

Footnote: *While Aphantasia certainly can be considered a neutral form of neurodivergence, with the brain spec'ced for non-visual thought processes, the woman in this tale does not consider herself to be on the Neurodivergent spectrum, given that she acquired the condition through brain damage from experimental tech (clues 3 and 12).

Turn the following page for solutions

A LOGICAL FUTURE

a logic puzzle by
Arlylic Killingstad

CATEGORY ICONS

- FEMALE
- MALE
- HOUSE
- TECH
- WRITER
- ARTIST
- NEURO-DIVERGENT

Entry forms (repeated)

- NAME:
- CAREER:
- CONDITION:
- PROBLEM:
- OUTCOME:

Grid labels

Careers: Game Designer, Pixel Artist, Storyboard Artist, Webcomic Artist, Novelist, Screenwriter, Journalist, Video Reviewer

CONDITIONS: ADHD, Autism, Dyslexia, Anxiety, Aphantasia, Cleithro, Insomnia, Visual Imp.

PROBLEMS: Plagiarism, AI Replaced, Bot Theft, Copyright, Fake News, Market, Predictive, Rumor of AI

OUTCOMES: Hammock, Hydroponics, Roommates, Hovercar, Emo Reg, Sell Memory, Dreamstate, Bought Out

Names: Ailana, Aleksandra, Emlyn, Kalino, Nicola, Milja, Seong-Su, Taizeen

Full labels (bottom)

Conditions: ADHD, Autism, Dyslexia, Anxiety Attacks, Aphantasia, Cleithrophobia, Insomnia, Visual Impairment

Problems: Acused of Plagiarism, AI Replacement, Bot Theft, Copyright Strikes, Fake News, Market Oversaturation, Predictive Algorithms, Rumor of AI Gen

Outcomes: Hammock Haven, Hydroponics Helper, Robot Roommates, Hovercar Homeless, Emotion Regulator, Selling Memories, Waking Dreamstate, Bought Out by DS

Careers: Game Designer, Pixel Artist, Storyboard Artist, Webcomic Artist, Novelist, Screenwriter, Journalist, Video Reviewer

A LOGICAL FUTURE: SOLUTION RUNDOWN

There are five women and three men (clues 1 and 2), of which three are writers and three artists (clue 4); two of each are female (clue 2), so one of each is male. This leaves two roles that aren't writers or artists (video reviewer and game designer), of which one is male and the other female. These basics are pre-marked on the chart for your convenience.

Taizeen and Kalino aren't artists (clue 4), so Seong-Su must be. Kalino can't get his engaging stories published (clue 8), so he's a writer (of fiction, not the journalist), leaving Taizeen.

Per clue 11, the game designer is male (hence Taizeen); he runs a small indie company making games for visually impaired players, but sales tanked due to market oversaturation. He had to sell his company (clue 1) to Discosoft Studios (clue 9). And he's visually impaired (still clue 9).

The rest of the creators are split into tech issues and housing issues; the former are all female (clue 12), so the housing issues are split evenly (two men and two women). The one living out of a hovercar is female (clue 7), as is the one with roommates (clue 10), so the other two must be Kalino and Seong-Su, who are living with family: a brother and an aunt (clue 7). Kalino has a brother (clue 8), while the one helping his aunt is an artist (clue 7), thus confirmed as Seong-Su.

Since Kalino has a supportive brother, he's not the screenwriter (clue 5), so he's the novelist, and has ADHD. He can't get published thanks to predictive algorithms (clue 8), so he's been living in a hammock in his brother's micro-apartment (clues 7 and 1).

Seong-Su must be the one who quit his job (clue 1) in protest over being replaced by AI (clue 9), so he's the storyboard artist. He's helping his aunt with her hydroponics farm (clue 7), but as the artist living with family, he has cleithrophobia (clue 6), which makes his undersea abode rather trying. (For those who didn't look it up, the phobias mentioned in clue 6 are, respectively, the fear of being trapped and the fear of deep water.)

That leaves the women: the video reviewer, plus two writers and two artists. The three who used risky tech don't include Nicola or Ailana (clue 4), so they must be Milja, Emlyn, and Aleksandra.

Nicola and Ailana, then, are the two with housing issues, both Neurodivergent (clue 2), who are thus Autistic and Dyslexic*, in some order (clue 4).

Aleksandra is a writer but not the screenwriter (clue 5); she's the journalist who overworked herself to the point of insomnia (still clue 5) fighting a flood of fake news (clue 1), and got a black-market sleep aid that started to trigger dream states while she was awake (clue 12).

The artist with an anxiety disorder doesn't start with a vowel (clue 3), and since she used a brain implant (clue 12), she can't be Nicola, so she must be Milja. She's not Neurodivergent, so she's not the Autistic artist (clue 6) and must be the pixel artist who got started with fan art. She got harassed over a rumor (clue 3) that her art was AI-generated (clue 2), and the resultant anxiety attacks led her to accept an emotion regulator (clue 12) that has sadly dulled her emotions and her ability to find joy in art.

The three women remaining are Ailana, Emlyn, and Nicola, who are, in some order, the Autistic artist (clue 6), the screenwriter (clue 5), and the video reviewer. Since neither Nicola nor Ailana used risky tech, it must be Emlyn who got brain damage leading to aphantasia while trying to sell copies of her memories to make ends meet (clue 12). She's not Neurodivergent (clue 2), nor a writer (clue 4), so she's the video reviewer; per clue 3, she's also the one hit by algorithmic copyright strikes.

The final artist is the webcomic artist, popular enough to make an income selling merch (clue 1); she's also the Autistic artist who needs a quiet environment (clue 6), but unfortunately had her art stolen by bots (clue 10), which presumably ate into her profit enough that she struggled to make rent, hence why she placed an ad for roommates (clue 7), who unfortunately turned out to be android adbots routinely advertising the very sites that facilitated the theft (clue 10 again).

Since the one living out of her hovercar isn't Ailana (clue 7), that must be Nicola, and Ailana is the Autistic artist (how alliterative!). Nicola, then, is the screenwriter accused of plagiarism by a faulty algorithm (clue 2), who, by process of elimination, is Dyslexic.

SOLUTION ON NEXT PAGE

	CAREER	CONDITION	PROBLEM	OUTCOME
AILANA	Webcomic Artist	Autism	Bot Theft	Robot Roomates
ALEKSANDRA	Journalist	Insomnia	Fake News	Waking Dreams
EMLYN	Video Reviewer	Aphantasia	Copyright Strikes	Selling Memories
KALINO	Novelist	ADHD	Predictive Algorithms	Hammock
MILJA	Pixel Artist	Anxiety Attacks	Rumor of AI Gen	Emotion Reg.
NICOLA	Screenwriter	Dyslexia	Plagiarism Accusation	Hovercar Home
SEONG-SU	Storyboard Artist	Cleithrophobia	Replaced by AI	Hydroponics
TAIZEEN	Game Designer	Visual Impairment	Market Over-saturation	Sold to Discosoft

||||||||||||||||||||||||||||||||||||||||||||||||||||||||||||||||||||||||||||||||||||||||||||||||||||||||||||||||||

CONTENT WARNINGS

Being a work of mature Horror, a degree of violence, gore, sex and/or death is to be expected in the stories contained in THANK YOU FOR JOINING THE ALGORITHM.

For more specific concerns, please check the list of stories below
for specific content warnings:

The Grid: bodily fluids, self-harm

Wound Together: self-destructive behavior

Please Rate Your Experience From 1-10: suicide

Please be advised. More information at www.tenebrouspress.com.

Printed in the USA
CPSIA information can be obtained
at www.ICGtesting.com
JSHW060931031223
52749JS00026B/53